THE MAKER
OF
MONSTERS

LORRAINE GREGORY

OXFORD
UNIVERSITY PRESS

1

It won't be like this for ever.

That's what I keep telling myself.

However bad it might be now, working from dusk till dawn in a mouldering old castle in the middle of the sea, one day it will all be different. It has to be.

One day I'll make my master proud of me. One day he'll give up his experiments and leave his laboratory and come outside again. Maybe he'll even smile at me the way he used to and ruffle my hair and tell me I'm like the son he never had . . .

'Brat! You useless, malingering fool, where are you?'

Judging by the high level of burning rage in his voice, I'd say today is not going to be that day.

I shove the huge pile of rotten meat I've been chopping into the wheelbarrow and hurry towards the door, my arms straining from the weight.

'BRAT!' My master roars again, and I can imagine the vein on his forehead bulging with fury.

'I'm coming!' I shout back, acid bubbling in my belly, wishing I wasn't so slow and useless and pushing the barrow even faster.

I'm almost at the door when I remember I need my keys. They're not on the table where I left them, or on the sideboard. It doesn't make any sense unless . . .

'Sherman!' I shout. 'Sherman, have you stolen my keys again?'

I get down on my knees and poke my head under the oven.

Sherman sits in his nest of old rags, his big heavy turtle shell covering his squat bristly boar's body and mismatched lizard legs.

'I need my keys, Sherman.'

Round eyes blink slowly at me from his wrinkled lizard face.

'Please Sherman, I'll be late,' I plead.

'Brat work too hard,' he says, gruff and stubborn as always.

'I do not! I'm fine,' I insist. 'And I'll get in trouble with Lord Macawber if I'm any later. Please!'

Sherman grunts and shifts his heavy body so I can see my ring of keys hidden in his nest. I breathe a sigh of relief.

'Thank you, Sherman. I'll see you later when I finish work. We can play then, all right?'

He snorts. I've made that promise before but I'm always so tired by the end of the day I end up falling asleep in front of the fire.

'BRAT!'

I jerk at my master's summons and bang my head on the metal oven rim. Swearing under my breath, I snatch up my keys, clip them to my belt, grab the wheelbarrow, and half run along the hallway and through the open door that leads down into the basement.

The sloping path is made of rough stone and twists around the centre of the tower in a narrow spiral. My overloaded barrow wobbles and squeaks on the way down.

'Where are you, boy?' Lord Macawber bellows again from his laboratory below. 'I need you here now.'

'I'm just going down to feed the creatures on level four,' I call back.

'You mean you haven't fed them yet? Great giblets, boy, could you be any more useless?' His voice is loaded with disappointment.

'I'm sorry, my lord. I'll be as quick as I can, I promise.'

He doesn't bother replying. He knows as well as I the consequences of letting the monsters on level four get too hungry.

I pass his laboratory as quietly as possible. The path beyond grows dim, the torch lights in the walls gutter, growing weaker all the time because Lord Macawber is too busy to recharge them with the magic they need.

I'm forced to make my way in the near dark, heart thumping, nerves stretched and thin . . .

'RAH!'

I scream like a startled banshee as sharp claws rip into my shoulder and the barrow tips over, dumping its contents all over the slope. My feet slip and slide in the mess as I try to escape and I scrape all the skin off my knee on the rough wall.

It's almost a minute before my mind stops panicking enough to pick out the sound of Tingle's laughter and I come to a dizzy halt.

'Tingle! What are you doing, you great barnacle? You nearly gave me a heart seizure!'

Tingle claws her way up my back and settles on my shoulder.

'Yay! Tingle be very scary,' she tells me, puffing out her chest with pride.

'Tingle be massive pain in the bum,' I snap. 'Look at the mess you've made. And I've hurt my knee now.'

Tingle's furry little cat face peers at me with downcast eyes.

'Not Tingle fault. Sherman be saying Tingle not scary, so Tingle must prove she is very scary, no?'

'No! Tingle must ignore Sherman and stop being naughty.'

Tingle's long monkey tail wraps itself around my neck and she rubs her cheek against mine.

'Tingle not naughty Brat-Brat! Tingle never naughty. Sherman be very naughty for saying all those bad things about Tingle.'

I sigh and bend down to start scooping the offal back into the barrow, wincing at the sharp stinging in my knee.

'All right, trouble, I have to get back to work now so unless you want to come with me to feed the monsters . . . ?'

As expected Tingle leaps off my shoulder with a terrified squeak and disappears up the path.

With a loud huff I pick up the barrow and start pushing. The front wheel wobbles worse than ever, my knee throbs with pain, but I ignore it all and keep going.

It won't be like this for ever, I remind myself again. And again. And again . . .

When I finally reach level four I unlock the heavy wooden door, heave up the crossbar, and shove it open. A waft of stale air, heavy with musk, dung, and ammonia, greets me and makes my eyes sting and my belly heave.

I have to force myself to enter. Every instinct I've got is screaming at me to keep out, to turn round and run away but I can't. The monsters need to be fed, no matter how terrified I am. It's bad enough the wretched beasts are locked in cages, without starving them as well.

I concentrate everything on keeping the barrow straight. It's no easy task with a wobbly front wheel and a limp but the hungry eyes peering from the cages on either side keep me motivated.

Each giant cell houses a monster. A creature that crawled from my master's unhinged imagination and was stitched together from the parts of many different monsters, before being dragged back to life using the magical art of necromancy.

Well, my master calls it art.

It's more of a sickness if you ask me. But people can be cured from sickness can't they? They can get better. I've been trying to help my master recover but it's not easy. The disease has taken hold of him and turned his brain sour.

The creatures snarl and shriek when they smell the rotten meat. A variety of scaled and hairy arms with curved talons or sharp claws reach through the bars trying to snag their meal straight from the barrow.

They'd try to snag me too if they could but I worked out long ago that none of them can reach me if I stay slap bang in the middle. The wobbly front wheel is making it harder than ever but there's no room for mistakes on level four. Two and three are dangerous enough but four, four is a nightmare made real. (I try never to even think about what's kept on level five. I just throw some carcasses down there every week or so and slam the trapdoor shut again.)

I'm nearly at the end of the corridor now, where the empty troughs are piled. I try and ignore the ravenous eyes that follow me, the soft splatter of slobber that drips from their jowls, sliding over sharp ivory fangs desperate for flesh.

My flesh.

A shiver ripples down my spine but I keep moving. The sooner I feed them, the sooner I can escape.

I fill up the troughs with scoops of offal and slam them into place through the bars of their cages. The monsters tear into their meat like they've been starved for weeks and ignore me briefly while they eat. I hurry back down the corridor towards the door with my nice light barrow.

But something flies out of the third cage and hits the wobbly wheel. It falls off entirely and the cart lurches sideways. I go with it, crashing into the bars with a strangled scream as I'm snatched up by strong arms and held tight against the bars.

Noxious, foetid breath drifts from the mouth behind me; a calloused tongue licks my neck, making me shudder with disgust and horror.

'Let me go!' I yell. 'Let me go now! I'm warning you! Lord Macawber will be angry with you if you hurt me!'

The creature makes a strange noise. Is it laughing?

Panic pumps around my body, making me buck and squirm till I'm about to rip myself in two but it's no good. I can't escape his death grasp.

'If-if-if you eat me now there'll be n-n-no one left to feed you,' I warn him in desperation. 'You'll all starve to death!'

'Not if weeee esssscapess firsssst . . .' it hisses, squeezing my chest, crushing it against the bars, one clawed hand reaching for the keys attached to my belt as if this is all part of some fiendish plan.

The thought of all these monstrous creatures being let loose sends me flailing around like a fish on a hook. I search for something—anything—to help me and my bulging eyes fall on the guttering torch on the wall, just out of reach. I twist my tortured body as much as I can to get my fingers close enough but the pain in my chest is making me feel faint and there are black spots in front of my eyes.

Just when I think my bones will crack I make a huge, desperate effort and my fingers curve around the torch handle. I yank it off the wall and thrust the flames behind me.

The creature roars back in shock and drops me to the floor. I land on my bum with a hard thud and crawl away from the cages before finding my feet and rushing through the door to safety.

2

By the time I limp into the laboratory, I'm a sweat-soaked mess, breath rasping in my throat, body trembling with pain.

Lord Macawber barely even looks up from his bench.

'Finally,' he snaps. 'Sometimes I wonder why I ever bothered saving your useless hide—you're about as much help as a constipated frog.'

'I was attacked,' I gasp. 'One of your monsters tried to eat me!'

'Don't be ridiculous,' he says with a bored sniff. 'You'd never fit through the bars.'

I can feel my eyelids prickling, wishing desperately for some small sign that he cares.

'But they did Master, look!' I pull up my

tunic so he can see the purple and blue bruises already blossoming across my ribs, the faint claw marks scratched along my neck.

His pale-blue eyes run over my wounds with a cold glance.

'Oh do stop whining boy, it's just a few bruises,' he says, picking up his big silver needle and threading it with thick, black thread. 'If you get too close to the cages you're bound to incite them to violence. They're vicious animals—that's what they've been designed for.'

'But I didn't get too close! One of them laid a trap for me. Knocked the wheel off my barrow so I'd fall and be close enough to catch.'

My master looks up from his work, his interest aroused at last.

'Really?'

'Yes. These last creatures you've made are too clever, Master. They think ... they plan ...' I lower myself gently onto the rickety chair by the door before I fall down. 'It wanted my keys Master, it was planning to escape.'

Lord Macawber smiles—it gives his gaunt,

pale face a spark of life.

'I knew it! My skills have grown; my creations are becoming more sentient and deadly each time.' He says it as if it's a good thing. As if they're not dangerous enough already without adding cunning and conniving into the mix.

He stands up and hurries across the flagstone floor towards his glass shelves full of bottles and jars, his bloodstained apron flapping about his skinny frame.

'It is the brains I think. I finally have the right formula to soak them in . . . it stops them rotting and increases the activity in the neural pathways.'

He turns around with a dish full of pink brains floating in a lumpy purple liquid.

I wrinkle my nose and gag slightly but Lord Macawber doesn't even notice.

'My latest creature will have no equal. This brain is bigger and better than anything I've used before, the essence more concentrated. He'll be more than just a perfect killing machine—he'll have intelligence enough to plan an entire war campaign!'

I glance down at the long wooden workbench set along the wall. A white sheet covers the massive creature lying there, leaving only a half-attached ogre arm visible, but it's enough to send a cold trickle of fear rippling down my spine.

'Is it not becoming too dangerous to continue now, Master?' I ask.

'Pish posh!' He says, nervously tugging at the gold locket around his neck. 'I keep telling you there's no real danger, don't I? It's all under control. I give them life but I can take it away at any time.'

'I wish you would take it away then, and let the cursed creatures rest in peace,' I mutter under my breath.

'Oh really, Brat?' He turns on me, eyes narrow and cold. 'Is that what you think? You feel sorry for my creations do you?'

I start to sweat. I didn't mean for him to hear me. 'No, Master. Sorry, Master.'

'It's your fault those creatures are still locked up in cages, boy, not mine,' he says. 'You've done nothing but hold me back and slow me down since the day you started work.

If I had a proper, competent assistant my army would have been complete years ago. It's your fault my sweet daughter is still trapped in the City, your fault that traitor Karush is running the entire place! IT'S ALL YOUR FAULT!'

My knees start shaking when he shouts. I can't help it. I'm just praying he doesn't start throwing things again.

'It isn't easy creating an army this magnificent, you know!' His rant continues. 'Not for a hundred years has magic like this even been used. I work like a slave every day of my life and your constant whining and bleating is only making it harder!'

'Yes, Master,' I say keeping my eyes downcast. 'I'm sorry, Master.'

'You should be! Now get back to work and stop lollygagging, you useless cretin! The storeroom needs cleaning and I don't have all day to wait!'

I scurry past him and reach for my mop and bucket. I'm good for something at least.

I drag my aching body into the kitchen, rip

off my filthy apron, and plunge my hands into the rainwater barrel in the corner so I can scrub at my face and wash away the blood and guts plastered over me after three hours cleaning the floor, the walls, and the ceiling in the storeroom.

My master's preservation spell had failed and all the carcasses had putrefied overnight. I didn't dare ask him why he hadn't recharged the magic. Didn't dare do anything but scrub until it was spotless.

I slump down in the old leather armchair and dry my hair half-heartedly with an old towel.

'Brat-Brat!' Tingle flies into the room and leaps onto my lap, jumping up to lick my face with her sandpapery tongue.

Her obvious affection is like a balm, soothing my pain and easing the ache of loneliness that sits constantly in my chest. Lord Macawber might think Tingle and Sherman are just useless failed experiments but they are everything to me.

I stroke her soft tawny fur, my fingers scratching at the thick black stitches that circle her neck, her limbs, her tail, until she collapses in a heap and starts purring softly.

'Tingle very hungry, Brat-Brat!' she whines and my belly lets out a gurgle of agreement. 'Tingle need munchies.'

Sherman adds his thoughts with a snort and a grunt from under the oven.

We're all hungry but I know full well there's barely a crumb in the cupboards.

'We'll have to go out and fetch food from the garden,' I tell them.

'Yay! We go garden! We go play!' Tingle springs up, green eyes flashing with excitement and Sherman pokes his head out from his hiding place, his pink tongue flickering.

'All right then, let's go,' I say, groaning as I lever myself out of the chair and limp after Tingle and Sherman.

It's only a scrubby patch of land behind the tower, halfway up the rocky cliff we live on. The path down to it is overgrown and steep and each step hurts my ribs but it's good to be outside. As long as I keep my gaze far away from the rough grey water surrounding us, that is.

The gloom of my horrid morning lifts as Tingle and Sherman chase each other in the fresh sea air, their shrieks of enjoyment mixing with the sharp call of the seabirds as I raid their clifftop nests for a few eggs. Then Sherman helps me drag up the baskets that I baited last week and I find them full of crabs and lobsters, enough to last us a few days at least.

Tingle tugs at my trouser leg with her teeth until I play chase and I find laughter bubbling inside as she slips between my hands over and over. Finally, breathless and hot, I sit down on the grass and let her taunt Sherman instead.

I busy myself pulling a few vegetables from the soil, hoping to eke enough out for a decent supper, but I can't help notice that the magic is failing out here too. Each crop I harvest is smaller than the last and the apple tree that should be ripe with fruit by now is barren of leaves and turning grey.

It's no surprise really. Lord Macawber hasn't left his laboratory for the past year, ignoring everything but his ridiculous plan.

I'm not sure how much longer we'll be able to survive out here if he carries on like this.

I peer quickly across the ever-churning sea to the horizon but there's no sign of any ships. They used to come every few months on their way to the Spice Lands, bringing food supplies and sometimes the monster carcasses Lord Macawber was so desperate for. In return my master would use magic to repair their ships or put preservation spells on their holds, but he's refused so many of them this year they've stopped coming at all.

The only other source of food is over on the mainland but even if I was welcome there it's well beyond my reach. The narrow causeway of slippery stone is the only path and it's lashed by huge waves constantly, watery fingers desperately searching for more victims to drag down into its cold and murky depths.

I did try to cross it once, years ago, after Lord Macawber had lost his temper and thrown half his laboratory at me for breaking one of his precious glass jars. I barely made it a quarter of the way across before my head exploded with memories and everything that happened the night I lost my parents came flooding back. I was stuck out there on the rocks for hours, too terrified to move, till Tingle and Sherman helped me stagger back to land. I never tried again after that. Maybe I should have.

I'm happily distracted from that idea by my friends' raised voices.

'Tingle is too very scary! Tingle make Brat-Brat all fall down!'

'Tingle not scary. Tingle big baby!'

'Am not!'

The fun and games never lasts for long with those two. They always end up bickering but it's mainly background noise to me now. A comfort more than a trial. Giving the illusion I'm not entirely alone here, though it often feels like it deep in my heart.

My basket is full of food but I have no desire to go back inside. Instead I move over to the apple tree, rest my back against the trunk, and close my eyes, craving five minutes of peace before I'm forced to return to my never-ending duties.

'Sherman eat Tingle!' he growls.

'No!' Tingle shrieks, scrambles onto my shoulder and up into the tree. 'No eat Tingle!'

I open one weary eye and watch her prance along the branches.

'Be careful Tingle . . . those branches aren't very safe now.'

Tingle ignores me.

'Sherman can't catch Tingle. Sherman is too slow, Sherman is too stupid . . .' she chants, poking out her little pink tongue at a grumpy Sherman down below.

Sherman flicks out his own long sticky tongue and the end jabs Tingle firmly in the chest.

She overbalances, tips backwards, and falls, her tail grabbing onto a lower branch in a desperate bid to save herself.

The thick branch gives a sharp snap and collapses right on my head.

ᴵ ⁄ ⧵ ⁄ ⁄ ⁄ ⁄ ⁄ ⁄ ⁄ ⁄ ⁄

My parents drowned when I was little and I was washed up here on the shore. Lord Macawber saved my life and let me stay in the castle. He was grieving the death of his wife and missing his daughter at the time but he was kind to me despite his sadness, often reading me stories and carving me toys.

But then his terrible obsession to build an army he could use to gain revenge on Lord Karush and rescue his daughter took hold. He disappeared down into the catacombs that run deep under the castle to start his experiments.

Back then there was another servant who lived here. Marta did the cleaning and cooking but she didn't like me under her feet so I was alone most of the time. Craving company, I took to roaming around the castle, exploring every crumbling tower and tunnel, until I found my way down to my master's laboratory.

He put me to work at once, said I needed to start repaying the debt I owed him, but I didn't mind helping. I liked it. I was still only small but working for Lord Macawber was better than being alone and he was different in the beginning: kinder, gentler.

Sherman was his first attempt at putting different pieces of animals together and bringing them back to life. It was terrible and

Lord Macawber was furious with the result. He dumped Sherman in a box in the storeroom and left him there.

I used to sneak in and feed him. Spend ages just talking to him while he snuffled and grunted.

A few months later I found Tingle in the box with him and she crawled into my arms and trembled so much that I couldn't bear to leave her. I ended up taking the box back to my room and they've been mine ever since. My only friends in the world.

They argue and fight and add about a full tonne of trouble to my life but I wouldn't be without them. Not ever. They're all I have.

It doesn't mean I'm not ready to wring their necks when I open my eyes and see them both peering at me.

I groan and sit up and everything goes a bit hazy.

'Brat?' Tingle whispers. 'Brat-Brat? We sorry, Brat-Brat.'

I reach one hand carefully up to my head and find an egg-shaped lump in the middle that's too sore to touch.

'What happened?' Sherman demands.

'You two tried to brain me with a branch, that's what happened!' I hiss through gritted teeth.

'No. What happen there?' Sherman's nose pushes against my ribs. They flame bright blue with bruises where my tunic's ridden up.

I pull it down quickly. 'Don't worry Sherman. It's fine. One of the creatures tried to eat me this morning, that's all. Obviously it must be let's-all-try-and-kill-Brat day!'

'No!' Tingle sneaks into my lap and covers my face in licks. 'Tingle love Brat-Brat!'

Sherman rarely says the words but he rubs his head against my leg to show his affection.

'Well . . . I suppose I love you both too,' I admit. 'Although to be fair it could be the bump on my head talking.'

'No bump! Brat love Tingle very much and Tingle kill those big bad meanie stinkers for hurting my Brat-Brat!' she says with a tiny, adorable growl.

'Well, I'd rather you tried to kill them than me, if you don't mind.' I stroke her soft fur with one hand.

'Macawber is bad man,' Sherman grumbles. 'Very dangerous. Not safe here.'

'I know,' I agree, stroking Sherman with my other hand, just under his neck where his heavy shell rubs. 'But he's sick isn't he? He needs our help to get better and you know it won't . . .'

'Be like this for ever.' Tingle and Sherman finish my sentence together. I guess I've said it a few times over the years. Whenever they start talking like this and trying to convince me to leave.

I've told them there's nowhere to go anyway.

After I ran away that time, Lord Macawber told me what happened to the mainland and why I could never go there. A terrible Mage War over a century ago had ravaged Niyandi Mor and turned it into a wasteland. The great Domed City Lord Macawber was banished from is the only safe place to live but its huge walls are fortified by magic and impossible to penetrate. The few people cast out beyond the city walls barely survive and would hardly welcome a useless boy and his freakish friends. We've no choice but to make the best of it here.

'Well, it won't be like this for ever!' I insist.

'Maybe not stay like this,' Sherman says. 'Maybe it get worse.'

He settles his hard head on my sore knee. Tingle presses my bruised ribs with her paws as she tries to find a comfy spot to sleep.

I want to ignore Sherman's prophecy of doom but I have a horrible feeling deep down inside that he might be right. If only Lord Macawber would realize that he doesn't need to smash down any walls to find a child to love.

I'm already here.

3

I leave Tingle and Sherman snoozing in bed where they've collapsed after their huge supper and take my master some of the leftover soup.

It's good. Made with the fresh crab and vegetables from the garden. I'm hoping it will soothe him enough to listen to me. We can't carry on like this, not after today. How can I ever go back down to level four? What if they try again? What if I can't stop them the next time? It's been seven years now since he began making monsters and I'm so tired of being afraid all the time.

'Master?' I call, walking carefully into the darkened laboratory and putting the tray down on the table. 'I have some supper for you.'

The sound of desperate sobbing fills the

room.

'Master?' I find him crying over his latest creation, lying still, and yet somehow still menacing, under the sheet. 'What's wrong?'

'It didn't work, Brat. I tried everything and I couldn't do it! My magnificent creature won't rise!'

Relief rushes through me but I'm careful not to show it.

'Never mind. You can always try another time when you've had more rest, Master. When you're feeling better, stronger.'

'But . . . he has to rise! He has to! I must get to Ellari, I must save her!'

'Come on now, you need to keep your strength up. I've made some lovely soup.' I lead him away from his monster and settle him into a chair.

'Yes . . . yes you're right,' he says. 'I can always try again tomorrow, can't I?'

'Yes, Master.' I agree with him but in my heart I'm thinking this is perfect timing. Maybe I can use his failure to finally convince him to think again.

I sit down next to him and patiently spoon

the soup into his mouth. He opens his mouth like a baby gull and swallows, once, twice, three times and then grabs my arm, staring at me as if he's seeing me for the first time.

'I shouldn't have shouted at you,' he says suddenly. 'You're a good boy really, you look after me and I do nothing but shout and rage. I'm sorry, Brat. I'm sorry you were hurt. Are you all right now?'

'I'm fine,' I tell him, savouring every soft word, every sign that the man I once knew is still inside. I can save him, I know I can and we can have a different, better future.

He calms a little and takes some more soup.

'I miss her,' he says, his voice dripping with grief.

'I know you do.'

He fumbles at his neck for the locket. I help him open the catch so he can see the miniature portrait of his daughter, a pretty girl with fair hair and dark, mischievous eyes. He strokes it with one finger, tears rolling freely down his cheeks.

A sharp stab of jealousy spasms in my chest. I wish he would look at me like that just once.

'I have to get to her. I have to tell her I'm sorry, I'm so sorry. I should never have let Karush take her. He said it was for her own good but he just wanted to hurt me.

'As if I wasn't hurt enough, losing my wife to the cursed pox! I hardly knew what I was doing when I tried to bring her back with necromancy. I was mad with grief, I didn't deserve to be treated like a monster and banished from my own home for life!'

'Don't worry about all that now,' I say.

'But what will I do, Brat? If I can't wake my greatest creation, what shall I do?'

'You could stop, Master,' I say, trying to keep my tone light, trying not to sound desperate. 'You could release all the creatures from their bondage and let them rest in peace.'

He frowns at me. 'Stop? But . . .'

'Please, Master, it's enough now. Seven years of struggle is enough. You don't really want to let that army loose, do you? Imagine what they would do! You are a good man, a kind man, you don't want innocent people to be hurt, do you? Not really.'

'But what about my daughter, what about Ellari . . . ?'

'But she's safe where she is, Master. She probably has a good life in the City. You deserve some happiness too. You can have it if you would only let go of this obsession! We could be happy here, couldn't we, Master? We were once. Do you remember?'

He looks at me, a tiny smile lifts the corners of his mouth. 'You liked my stories . . .' he says slowly.

'Yes!' I grip his hand. He's listening to me. He's actually listening! 'Life could be good again. Ellari doesn't need you any more, she's sixteen now, all grown up.'

'But what about Karush . . . what about what he did to me? He must be punished!'

'But the only one being punished all these years is you!' I insist. 'You spend every minute working, you barely eat or sleep, you haven't been outside in over a year, and you're angry all the time.'

He sighs. 'Yes . . . you may be right. This isn't any way to live, for either of us. I don't know what I've been thinking.'

'It's all right, Master. You were grieving, you didn't mean it, but now you can stop and we can start again.'

Lord Macawber nods slowly. 'Start again. Yes, that's what we'll do. I am tired of this life Brat, so tired.'

I want to jump up and shout with joy but I don't want to break the spell.

'Why don't you sleep now, Master? We can talk again tomorrow when you're rested.' I help him up and lead him over to the couch. He lies down and lets me cover him with a blanket.

He grips my hand in his. 'Don't ever leave me, Brat. Please.'

'I'm not going anywhere, Master.' I sit down on the edge of the couch and let him keep hold of my hand. Slowly his eyes close and his breathing deepens but his grip on my hand never falters.

I spend ages savouring his words, imagining our future together, free from his obsession, a warm feeling spreading through me until finally, I doze off by his side.

4

'Ha! I did it!' My master's jubilant voice drags me awake.

'What?'

'You were right, Brat,' he says. 'I just needed food and rest and now it's done. He wakes at last.'

Still groggy with sleep, I turn my head to see what he means and my jaw falls open at the sight that greets me.

I watch the beast rise slowly from the table and stand on two mighty lionus legs, strong enough to bear the weight of the huge black-bear torso attached on top with rows of thick black stitches. Two massive ogre arms dangle on either side, each fingernail embedded with a razor-sharp eagle claw. Bringing the creature up to ceiling height is the rare and formidable head of a vicious gatorica lizard.

Lord Macawber has truly outdone himself this time. All his years of practice, perfecting his technique, combining the right pieces, had paid off. It's the most terrifying masterpiece of a creature I've ever seen.

'No,' I breathe into the chill air. 'You said you'd stop, you said!'

But Lord Macawber isn't listening to me. He's walking towards his enormous monstrous creation with a face as rapt as a new father gazing upon his firstborn.

'Greetings!' my master calls. 'I am Lord Macawber. I am your maker and you must hear me. I have brought you back to life for one purpose. To destroy the Domed City and bring me the head of Mulligan Karush!'

My master carries on talking, caught up in his favourite tale, even though the creature barely seems to know he's there.

'Mulligan Karush is a traitor and a coward and a thief! He banished me here to this barren rock and stole my only daughter from me but after many years of toil I will have my revenge at last. You, my mighty general, will lead the army of creatures waiting below and fulfil my promise!'

The creature clutches at his head with his huge hands and lets out a blood-freezing cry, showing off the many rows of enormous serrated white teeth that fill his massive jaws.

'You will follow my orders or suffer the consequences!' Lord Macawber insists, holding his locket with one hand and extending his other palm out towards his creation.

The monster shakes his head wildly from side to side as if demons are eating at his brain, its eyes deep black pools of nothingness. It starts lashing out with his mighty arms.

Shelves smash, tables fly across the room, glass rains down on us as the monster seems to lose all control. I dive behind the couch to avoid the falling debris.

'STOP!' Lord Macawber bellows. 'I am your master, you must obey me.'

I peek up over the edge and see the creature snatch Macawber up in one great fist.

'WRATH HAS NO MASTER!' he bellows into his face before hurling him across the room and continuing his destruction.

I watch Lord Macawber's body smash into the opposite wall by the door with a heavy thud and slide slowly down. He lies unmoving on the floor like a broken doll and I have to bite my tongue to stop from screaming his name.

I take a deep breath and crawl to him as fast as I can. Making my way around the edge of the room, dodging the glass shards scattered all over the floor, and hiding each time the monster's gaze turns my way.

'Master,' I whisper when I'm close enough, tucked away behind an overturned chair. 'Master?'

He has to be all right. He must be.

'Master, please!' I hiss. His eyes jerk open, dazed and wide with pain and shock.

'Brat?'

'Yes, it's me, I'm here. Are you all right?'

'No . . . I can't get up. Something's broken . . . inside.'

This is bad. So bad. And I can't help him while that monster is on the loose.

'You have to stop the monster, Master. Do it now.'

'I can't stop him!' he snaps. 'You saw me try and use the locket . . . nothing happened. I can't activate it now that my magic is gone.'

'Gone?' I gasp. 'How can it be gone?'

'Magic isn't infinite, Brat. We all have limits and necromancy stretches it much further than the other arts. Raising that creature drained the last of it and now . . . now I'm useless.'

With a horrible sinking feeling I remember the uncharged torch lights, the barren garden, the failed preservation spell in the storeroom.

'You knew, didn't you? You knew you were running out of magic but you raised that monster anyway! Even though you just told me you'd stop!'

'You don't understand! It was my last chance, I had to do it, boy! I couldn't let Karush get away with it, could I?'

I feel sick. The last shred of love and trust I had for him shrivels up inside me.

'You risked us all, everyone, knowing you might not have enough magic left to stop them, all so you could get your stupid revenge?'

'He deserves it!' Lord Macawber snarls. 'They

all do, the whole city! How dare they banish me after everything I did for them?' He coughs and the pain makes him wince and groan.

'You fool. You selfish, miserable fool!' I want to beat him with my fists. I don't want to die. Not here, not like this.

'Well, it's done now and so am I,' he says, his voice bitter with failure.

'And so are we all!' I hiss. 'That monster you just made will release the army below and destroy everyone. You know he will! And your precious daughter won't be safe either!'

His eyes widen. He swallows. As if this realization has only just occurred to him.

'There might still be a chance,' he says, thrusting the locket into my hands. 'Take it to Ellari, she's the only one who can activate it now, her blood is mine. She can use it to drain the magic that drives them.'

I shake my head wildly. 'What? Are you mad? How am I supposed to escape the castle and cross the water? Let alone travel across the wastes and get into the Domed City to find your precious daughter!'

Cabinets smash over our heads and shards

of wood shower us. The creature shows no sign of ending his rage but his move into the store room gives us a brief respite.

'You must find a way. I'm sorry, sorry for all of it, but there's no other choice. It all rests on you now.'

'No . . .' My voice is small. Small and afraid.

'Yes. I have faith in you, Brat, you're far stronger than you realize.'

But I'm not, I want to shout. I'm not.

'And when you find her, tell Ellari I'm sorry . . .' he says, swallowing hard. 'Now go, quick, he's coming back.'

I don't know what to do. I feel sick and hot and dizzy but there's no time to waste on feelings. This isn't just about me. I brush the tears away with my sleeve and start crawling, the locket clutched tightly in my hand.

When I reach the doorway I turn back for one last look at my master, cowering under the looming shadow of his final creation as it bears down on him.

And then I keep moving, leaving Macawber to his awful, bitter fate.

5

My heart is pounding in my chest as I run blindly down the corridor.

The other creatures are howling excitedly in their cages, the stink of fresh blood rousing their predatory instincts and hammering home the horrific danger surrounding me.

I have to leave. Right now.

But I'm not going anywhere without my friends. I have lost enough for one day.

I run on wobbly legs out of the basement and up the stairs, wishing I had never woken up, wishing this whole nightmare away.

'Tingle!' I shout, throwing open the door to my chamber. 'Sherman!'

I can't see them. They're not in the bed. They're not in the room.

'Where are you?'

I can't lose them. I can't. They're my family. They're all I have. I open the wardrobe, check under the bed.

'Tingle, Sherman, please come out. We have to go now!'

'Brat-Brat?' Tingle's voice emerges from the corner where she's huddled up against Sherman under the table. 'Tingle not like the loud noise, Brat-Brat. Tingle hiding.'

Relief fills me. 'I know. It's all right now, I'm here but we have to go. It's not safe here any more.'

'Never been safe,' Sherman mutters.

He's right. Macawber's been playing with fire for years and now the whole world might just burn.

I take a deep breath and try and shut out the rising panic so I can think. Try to plan. Try not to mess it all up . . .

Whatever they might think of me I owe the people on the mainland some warning of what's coming.

We have to get out of the castle before the monsters find us and get down to the beach where the causeway runs across the sea. I can worry about actually crossing the cursed thing if we make it out of here alive.

'Let's go,' I say as firmly as I can, leading my friends down the stairs towards the back door that leads to the cliff path. Sherman's short lizard legs and heavy shell make it hard for him to move fast so I heave him up into my arms. Despite the danger he isn't best pleased at the indignity and huffs loudly at me when I put him down again at the bottom.

The whole ground floor of the castle is filled with roaring and screeching and the sounds of destruction as the caged beasts are freed and make their way up out of the old catacombs.

Tingle climbs up my leg and wraps herself round my neck, her small body trembling as we carefully make our way in the shadows to the great hall where the back door is.

But the huge space is already crammed full of War Creatures. They're lined up in ranks already, like a proper army. The true depth of the danger we've let loose upon the world starts to sink in.

Before I can turn and run more creatures begin to arrive so I duck behind the door and hide in the shadows, unable to stop staring at the results of my master's obsession.

The heaviest, strongest monsters from level three are at the front; sewn together from pieces of trolls, steel-horn rhinos, Borvon bears, gorillicas, and moon-herd buffalo.

Behind them in the next row stand the level four beasts. A mixture of Parthernan wildcats, ogres, swamp hogs, Hibernan ice bears and green scaled drakin lizards. Their vicious claws and teeth ready to rend and tear at the enemy.

Arrayed along the sides are the inhabitants of level two; fast pack animals, combinations of hyper wolves, razorback boars, and demon panthers.

The creatures from level five have yet to arrive, still struggling to escape from their deep dark tunnels probably, and for that at least I'm grateful. I'm already too scared to move. There's enough brute strength and malevolent rage in this room to destroy half the world without adding in the dark and festering beasts from below.

Luckily, none of them notice me hiding. Their attention is fully caught by him.

Wrath.

My master's greatest creation. He stands on the raised dais at the other end of the hall, his magnificent terribleness turning my legs to jellified goo. I see now that his eyes are not truly black at all but stained the rich, dark crimson of fresh blood.

A roar rises from his throat, silencing the creatures before him.

'My brothers and sisters! We have been wronged! Dragged back from death, locked away in cages, denied our freedom! But I, Wrath, have freed you! Now we shall begin our true purpose!'

His army bellow and hoot their approval.

'They call us War Creatures so it is war we will bring them! A war on all mankind. We will march to their city and crush the last of these meddlesome humans beneath our feet! We will bathe the ground in rivers of blood and we will not rest until death reigns eternal!'

The hall erupts with even more noise. Their sudden freedom combined with the promise of a chance to run amok has filled them all with an uncontrollable glee.

This might be the time to move, while their attention is fixed on Wrath and I have some small chance of escape. I tiptoe forward slowly but a heavy drakin lizard tail swings wildly in excitement and nearly hits me. I jerk backwards to avoid it, fall over Sherman, and land with a noisy splat on the stone floor.

The entire army of War Creatures turns to stare at me.

'Who are you, boy?' Wrath is a fitting name for him. His reptilian gaze locks me in place, sending fear through my very marrow.

I can't speak. I can't do anything.

'It isss the one who bringss ussss our rotten meat.' The voice of the gruesome creature from level four that attacked me rises into the hall.

I freeze for a moment while Wrath's scarlet pupils burn into mine, my breath coming in short gasps.

Wrath licks his lips with a dark black tongue.

'Rotten meat?' he says, looking me up and down like a wolf hunting a young deer. 'I say we deserve fresh meat!'

The monsters let out a wild baying, desperate for my blood.

'Let meeee have him, Masssster? I have tassssted his sweeeet flesh before,' the creature from cage three begs, drool spilling from his jaws.

'A hunt then, to celebrate our freedom! You may have first try but let the boy run awhile, his fear will only make his flesh sweeter!'

Tingle's terrified mew in my ear breaks me out of my trance and I scramble to my feet and flee, the heavy rumble of Wrath's laughter following behind us like a cloud.

6

We are prey now.

Hunted.

The terror of it gives wings to our feet, even Sherman's, as we flee back the way we came and up the stairs.

I take the third corridor, dash the length of it, turn right, and pelt down the stone steps to the old armoury that sits above the main hall.

Maybe we can climb down the outside of the castle? Maybe there's a rope or something in here that I can use to lower Tingle and Sherman?

I search through the cupboards furiously; none of them are full of weapons and supplies of course but all manner of useless junk instead. We have to get to that beach somehow though. The castle holds only death for us now.

'Meanie stinker, Brat-Brat!' Tingle screeches and I spin round.

The creature from level four strides into the room and I stumble backwards as his true hideous form becomes clear in the light. Its lower torso and legs come from a huge fleshy ogre, and clumps of wiry black hair and enormous warts sprout all over the thick, wrinkled skin. His upper torso, arms, and head come from the enormous green-scaled drakin lizard; muscled, vicious, and deadly. He fills the entire chamber with menace, drool dripping from his tooth-rimmed jaw.

I gulp down my terror and keep my eyes fixed on him as I move slowly around the room, my brain frantically trying to think of an escape.

'Nowheressss to ruuuun now, boy,' he says, his narrow eyes tracking me like an eagle.

There's no way we can get past him. No way we can dodge those nine-inch claws. We're trapped.

I step backwards, feeling my way into the

empty wooden shelving unit, next to the metal pipe. The faint beginnings of a ridiculous plan are starting to form.

The creature prowls closer, ready to strike.

'Go 'way, meanie stinker!' Tingle shouts, her fur puffed out like a ball around her.

As soon as his gaze strays from me I push the bottom section of pipe with my foot so that it faces away from us and towards the beast.

'I will pickkkk your bonesss from my teethhh,' the monster growls at Tingle, snapping his jaws together. She shrieks and claws her way up my leg and into my arms.

Sherman moves in front of us both and sets his shell down firmly.

'If you have any teeth left,' Sherman growls with a surprising amount of menace.

The War Creature laughs, baring his gleaming fangs at us. I slowly raise my hand to the lever on the wall behind me and when the laughter stops and he starts his charge, I yank down hard.

Cannonballs shoot from the end of the pipe and slam into the monster.

We don't get to watch because the hatch

under our feet disappears and we plunge down into a metal tube, sliding along its slippery surface in a confused tangle of arms, legs, tail, and shell.

The tube ends suddenly and now we're simply falling. It crosses my mind that maybe I hadn't thought this through properly when we land on damp sand with a painful, jarring thud.

'Yay!' Tingle shouts, jumping up and scampering around on top of me and Sherman. 'We go again-again?'

Only her paws landing on a particularly sensitive spot get me up on my feet. That and the need to check that we're not being followed. I'm pretty sure that creature would never fit down the tunnel, but better to be safe than squashed by a monster, I say.

When I've reassured myself that it's not following us I let out a breath.

'Tingle like slidey!' she says, scampering along the small beach, the full moon shining down on her footsteps.

'It's not exactly a slide, Tingle. It's a special trap in case the castle is attacked by pirates.

The cannonballs were supposed to fall down that tube and squash them but I made a few changes.'

'Brat-Brat very clever!' she says.

'Or very lucky,' Sherman grumbles, shaking sand out of his shell.

'Definitely lucky. I used to play in there when I was little and always wanted to try it out for real but I can't believe it actually worked.'

'We cross the bridge now, Brat-Brat?' Tingle asks, skipping in and out of the waves near the causeway.

I look out at the thin strip of rock running a mile or more across the sea to the mainland, nerves cramping at my belly. Can I really do this?

'We must go now, Brat, warn people.' Sherman says, his voice firm.

He's right. Of course he's right. I know there are people living on the other side. Sometimes on a clear day I see them fishing, and once or twice when the wind is right I've heard music and laughter, children playing ... they won't welcome me of course, or my news, but it has to be done.

I gulp. My head is hurting. All I can imagine are the waves snatching at my feet as I cross, the cold murky depths waiting to claim me, just as they did my ma and pa.

Heart thumping, fear swallowing me up, throat closing, I stagger away from the creeping tide.

'I can't do it . . . I can't cross . . . the water . . .'

'Brat must be brave,' Sherman says. 'No choice.'

'I CAN'T!' I shout. I turn away from his accusing eyes. I know I'm a coward. I know it and I hate it but I can't help it.

'Don't be 'fraid, Brat-Brat. Tingle help.' She curves her way up and around my neck to lick my ear.

'We keep you safe, just like last time,' Sherman says. 'Promise.'

I bite my lip.

There isn't much time. Soon the tide will rise to cover the causeway entirely. Soon any chance of warning the innocent people across the sea of the monstrous army heading their way will be gone. And when the sun rises and the tide lowers once more, they'll die. All of them.

And it will be all my fault. Lord Macawber always said I was useless and he was right. I've been a fool. Helping him with his plan, believing his lies, thinking I could stop him, imagining he would ever care about me.

A fool, and as if that's not bad enough, a coward too. I can't even cross this cursed causeway and give the people on the mainland some chance to escape!

I grit my teeth and turn around to face Sherman. 'All right, I'll try.'

Sherman nods, a hint of pride shining in his eyes. 'Follow Sherman.'

I focus on his back as he walks across the sand and up onto the rocky path. I step where he steps. Not looking anywhere but at his wide green shell.

Sherman walks slowly, calmly, and Tingle stays warm and soft around my neck as I creep out onto the causeway.

The sound of the waves crashing against the rocks and the wet spray against my face make me freeze, but then Tingle starts talking. Her voice fills my ear, I don't listen to the words, just use her voice to drown out the terrifying roar of the sea. I keep walking.

I try not to think about the water surging on either side, try not to imagine the water rushing over my head and into my lungs and slowly dragging me down, down into the depths . . . into the darkness . . . into the endless nothing where my ma and pa are waiting for me . . . their hair floating like weeds in the sea . . .

'BRAT!'

Tingle's shrieking into my ear brings me back.

It happened again.

Just like the last time.

I find myself crouched on the rock, arms over my head, and I don't remember how I got here or how long it's been but the tide has risen and it's pooling around my feet now. I'm freezing cold and wet through but the sheer panic in Tingle's voice forces me to open my eyes.

'Tingle?'

'THEY COMING!' she yells from the

rocks behind me, her eyes wide with horror.

'Who is?'

'MEANIE STINKERS!'

I turn to look back at the castle but I can't see any giant monsters, can't see anything except shadows . . . big, black shadows crawling down the castle walls and across the beach and racing towards us.

My heart jerks in my chest as the realization sinks in.

The most terrible creatures of all, released from the dark and desperate depths of level five are here, and they're coming for us.

7

My terror of the sea is overwhelmed for an instant by my fear of the many-legged horrors currently heading our way. I stand up and start running along the causeway, my heart beating painfully in my chest.

My clogs slip and slide on the wet stones but somehow I manage to stay on my feet and keep going.

Tingle speeds ahead, her nimble paws easily navigating the wet path. Sherman is doing his best on his short legs but he's struggling to keep up and I overtake him easily. My instinct to keep running is so strong I almost keep going and leave him behind but I grip my terror by the neck and choke it.

While I stop and wait for Sherman to catch

up, I make the mistake of turning my head.

Six or seven giant mantis bodies scurry along the rock towards us on hairy, spiderish legs, their long, whip-like scorposa stingers dripping with green poison waving behind them.

Black beady eyes glisten wetly in their huge heads, reflecting my fear right back at me. Scissor-sharp mandibles taken from a giant tarantulus click-clack together as they approach.

Soon they'll be on us, their many legs will catch us up in minutes, and then they'll be slicing into our flesh with their jaws or stabbing their stingers into our bodies to fill them with venom . . .

I take a deep breath and heave Sherman up into my arms, fear giving me the strength to keep running, even though the waves are crashing and my feet are now sloshing through the chill and greedy sea.

'Leave me,' Sherman grumbles, struggling in my arms.

'Don't be silly,' I pant.

'Leave me, Brat. Sherman too slow, too

heavy, no use.'

'I'd never leave you, not ever. Now shut up and let me concentrate.'

I don't look behind again. My eyes stay fixed on the shore, the faint outline like a beacon in the moonlight.

I block out the sounds of the clacking legs and the roaring sea and listen to my heartbeat. To Sherman's steady breathing.

I keep moving, even when my arms and legs are burning and my lungs are ready to explode.

But deep in my heart I think it's too late, the creatures are too close and I'll never outrun them.

We're lost.

And if we are lost, then so are all the people on the other side.

'Brat-Brat!' Tingle's voice calls to me.

'Tingle? Where are you?' I can't see her ahead on the path. I can't see her anywhere.

'Here! Over here, Brat-Brat!'

I turn my head to follow the sound and I see a round shell of a boat riding the waves on our right. A vague figure is steering the boat closer with a long oar.

Tingle is gripping the edge and her eyes are wide with terror. I don't look back but I can feel the creatures' hungry breath fall hot and heavy on my neck, driving me on.

'Jump!' a voice calls. 'Now!'

The voice is so strong, so confident, that my brain reacts instantly and despite my fear I find myself leaping into the sea. Giant pincers snap shut over my head, missing me by inches.

I choke and gasp as the water covers me but a strong hand finds me and pulls me up so I can grasp the edge of the small boat. I shove Sherman up and he's hauled out of my arms.

A hissing comes from behind me, a pincer grabs my tunic and tries to yank me back.

Tingle shrieks.

I turn my head and see pitch-black jaws arcing towards my face.

I freeze in horror but a girl rises up in the boat and swings her oar wildly like a bat, slamming the creature in the face with a resounding wallop.

It falls back.

I'm dragged into the boat.

'Stay down,' the voice instructs and I'm happy to lie gasping on the floor of the boat as the girl paddles us away from the causeway and the creatures like a saviour from a fairy tale.

The round boat reaches land with a bump twenty minutes later and the girl jumps out and hauls it further up the shingle beach.

I climb out behind her, fall to my knees, and vomit up the gallons of seawater I swallowed. A wet, bedraggled Tingle leaps onto the edge of the boat and starts grooming her fur. Sherman has no choice but to wait for the girl to lift him out and dump him on the sand next to me.

'Well, you lot are the weirdest catch I've ever had and no mistake.' The girl stands with her hands on her hips and stares down at us. She's smaller than me but not much, dressed in ragged trousers and a mottled grey leather jerkin, and yet she fought off the monsters like a warrior.

'Are they gone? The monsters? Are they gone?' I ask, my eyes scanning the shoreline for any trace.

'I saw the waves take them under,' she says with a sniff, brushing back her short dark curls. 'They didn't look like the best swimmers to me so most likely they drowned. If they do turn up anywhere it'll be back at the Castle. Not here.'

I collapse on my back and stare up at the night sky, my heart rate slowly returning to normal. We're alive. And we're safe for a few hours at least.

'Thank you for helping us,' I tell the girl, feeling shy and awkward and even more useless than usual.

'Looked like you needed it,' she says, but she grins as she says it which takes the sting out a bit.

'Are you usually out on a boat in the middle of the night?' I ask, getting carefully to my feet.

She shrugs. 'Best time to put the nets out. The incoming tide brings lots of fish in and a few surprises too. Your little cat friend jumped in my boat and started talking. I thought I was dreaming for a minute till she licked my nose.'

'She does like doing that.'

'I'm Molly by the way. You're that boy from the Castle, aren't you?'

I nod. 'I'm Brat. You've already met Tingle and that's Sherman.'

She lowers her voice so they can't hear. 'What are they . . . exactly?'

'They're my friends. Lord Macawber made them but they won't hurt you.'

She nods, accepting my words more easily than I'd imagined. 'And the . . . things . . . chasing you?'

'War Creatures. My master made them too, stitched them together from the carcasses of other monsters to make them as frightening as possible. Then brought them to life using necromancy. They will definitely hurt you if they get the chance.'

'I figured that much out for myself.' She gazes over at the crumbling castle perched atop the thrusting rocky pinnacle. 'You know I always wondered what that crazy old man was up to. There were rumours about monsters but . . . we never expected this!'

'Everyone will know soon enough,' I tell her. 'As soon as the tide goes down in the morning there'll be a whole army of them heading this way.'

'You mean there are more? And why would your master send an army over?'

'He's not,' I tell her. 'He's dead. There's no one controlling them now.'

She lets out a long, low breath. 'So, what are we going to do?'

I shake my head, the enormity of it all crashing down on me. 'I have to get to the Domed City. It's our only hope.'

'Well, you can't go anywhere like that,' Molly says, looking at my soaking clothes. 'Let's get you back to the village first.'

'No, there's no time to stop!' I clamber to my feet. 'You go and warn the village, tell them to run away, to leave. I have to get to the City now before it's too late.'

'Don't be silly! You said yourself they can't cross until morning.'

'You don't understand. They'll kill everyone and it's all my fault!'

I start hurrying away down the beach but whatever was giving me energy disappears in a puff of smoke. My knees buckle and then my whole body starts trembling from shock and cold and I think it will never stop.

'You won't get anywhere like that, you big barnacle!' Molly says with a huff, wrapping a strong arm round my shoulders before I fall down entirely.

I feel so weak I have to give in. I let her lead me away, taking one last glance back at the castle over my shoulder.

I can just make out a seething mass of monstrous bodies, thronging the small beach, just waiting for the tide to recede and their hunt to begin.

The village is only a short walk over the beach and behind the dunes. Within minutes I'm dressed in dry clothes, wrapped in a blanket, and sat in front of a roaring fire with a hot cup of nettle tea while Molly tells everyone what happened.

The villagers, maybe sixty of them all together, not counting the sleeping children, are busy with their nets and boats but the news is spreading through the group and the noise is rising.

Tingle and Sherman have fallen fast asleep on my blanket and don't notice the strange looks they're getting.

I sip my tea, the shivering slowly subsides, and a warm sense of belonging seeps into my bones. This village, like their welcome, is not what I was expecting. Macawber led me to believe the villagers would reject me but they've welcomed me in. I don't imagine it will last if they realize the truth though.

The dozen or so dwellings have been crafted from the bones of some enormous sea creature and covered in the same grey leather as Molly's jerkin. They're set in a sheltered spot behind the dunes and the sea breeze is barely noticeable but it's a barren place. There are no trees or grass or anything much.

What they do have are more boats—coracles Molly called them—nets, woven baskets, and blankets. Everything is handmade from what I can tell, with just a few pieces of metal like the cooking pot over the fire and a few knives and spears.

My master told me the lives of the outcasts—those poor folk exiled from the Domed City—were difficult and that's obvious to see. But despite the harshness of their lives they have made a home here and it seems a far kinder one than Lord Macawber ever offered me. It occurs to me now that he was probably lying to me about them all along, to keep me slaving away by his side. If I'd been a touch braver then maybe I could have grown up here with Molly instead.

Finally one of the women, older than the others, with fine dark hair and kind eyes, comes to sit next to me.

'So, you're Brat, the orphan-boy Marta told us of.'

'Marta?' She'd left us five years ago without a word and her chores had become mine. 'Did she come here after?'

The woman nods. 'She was sick. Too sick to work any more. She told us some strange tales of what was going on up there before she died. We thought she was delirious but from what Molly tells me she just saw, Marta was telling the truth.' She shakes her head. 'Anyway, my name is Cassy. I am the clan mother here. I'm sorry we can't welcome you properly, as a guest should be welcomed, but it seems we have little time for the niceties.'

'You've been very kind, too kind,' I mumble, eyes lowered. 'I'm sorry to bring you this news, sorry for everything.'

'Don't be silly, we appreciate the warning. This monster army you speak of will cross at dawn, is that right?'

I nod. 'They'll cross as soon as the causeway is clear.'

'And do you know their plans?'

I take a deep breath. 'To bring death and destruction to the City and all humans.'

Cassy's face turns pale.

'So, we take to the water until they pass,' one of the men nearby interrupts. 'We can go in different directions and spread the word to the coastal villages as we go.'

'I need to get to the Domed City and warn

them of what's coming,' I say. 'Is there any way you can help me?'

Another man with a bushy black beard and a big barrel-shaped chest snorts loudly. 'Warn them? Why warn them? Let them all die I say.'

'Kendrick!' Cassy snaps. 'That is cruel.'

'Cruel? They happily sent us out here to die, we should return the favour. Why are we even waiting? Let's finish packing our things and ready the boats.'

I frown and Cassy catches my eye. 'He's right I'm afraid. We can't risk ourselves for the City. Chances are we wouldn't even make it there before this army caught us, and even if we did reach them, they wouldn't listen to us anyway.'

'But why not?'

'Because we are outcasts,' Cassy explains. 'They have convinced themselves we are worthless trash who lie and cheat and can't be trusted. It makes it easier for them to throw us out.'

'Besides,' Kendrick says. 'They have their stupid walls to protect them. What do we have?'

'But the only way to stop the monsters lies in the City,' I say. 'If they're not stopped you'll never be safe.'

'Then maybe it's time we left for good. Find a way to cross the reefs and seek a new home?' Kendrick says, his dark eyes drifting off to the horizon and the vague promise of safety.

'And just abandon everyone else?' I ask.

'They abandoned us first, boy!' He storms off, leaving an awkward silence around me and I wish the sand would devour me into its depths. I should have kept quiet. No one wants my opinion.

'What about Arberra?' Molly demands, her green eyes flashing in the firelight. 'Who's going to warn them?'

'Now Molly . . .' Cassy starts, holding her hands up.

'What?' She snaps. 'You're going to leave our own people to die too? Their settlement is closest to the City, they won't stand a chance!'

'Our people?' Cassy's jaw tightens. 'Those thieves and smugglers in Arberra are traitors.'

'You mean the people who take all the risks

dealing with the City so that we can survive out here?'

'Molly, I know how you feel but it's too dangerous. We're leaving, now, and that's the end of it.'

'Fine.' Molly storms off.

Cassy smiles down at me. 'Molly is a fiery soul. Don't worry. She knows this is for the best.'

'I'm really sorry . . . about everything,' I tell her. Guilt at the disaster I've helped unleash sits like a weight on my chest.

She smiles and wraps a warm arm around my shoulders. The motherly gesture sends a shaft of pain to my heart and fills me with a desperate longing for my own ma, lost so long ago I barely remember her.

I swallow it down.

'It's hardly your fault, is it? And we are grateful for your warning, Brat. It was very brave of you to come here.'

'Brave?' I shake my head. 'Me? No, I'm not brave . . . if it wasn't for Molly we'd all be dead.'

'Well, we're glad you're not!'

'Me too.' In fact I'm still rather surprised about the whole thing. Luck must have been on our side tonight. I only hope it holds out.

'You know, there's room for you in one of the boats if you want it? Come with us, you'd be welcome.'

'Really?' I'm so surprised by the offer I nearly spill my tea. My heart swells three sizes at the idea of being offered a place among these people. Maybe they would accept me even if they knew the truth?

'Your . . . friends . . . can't come though, lad,' she adds with a frightened glance at Tingle and Sherman. 'It's just . . . they're monsters too, aren't they? How can we trust they won't turn on us?'

9

I'm still sitting there in the first rays of dawn when Cassy and the boats leave.

Of course I am.

My legs are numb from the weight of my sleeping friends but I don't care. If they're not welcome then neither am I.

Besides, the thought of being in a tiny boat on the vast sea makes my throat close with terror.

Not that it's any safer here of course.

The War Creatures are coming. And the longer I sit here doing nothing the closer they'll get.

And yet, despite the imminent danger, I can't seem to move.

My mind is frozen.

Trapped in the net of my own uselessness.

How can I travel across the wastes on my own? I don't even know where the stupid City is! I don't know anything. I'm only good for scrubbing floors and shovelling dung and what use is that out here?

None.

We'd be dead already and the locket at the bottom of the sea if it wasn't for Molly and she's gone now.

'Brat-Brat!' Tingle says, opening her eyes and stretching.

I swipe away the rogue tears quickly. 'Morning, Tingle.'

She looks around at the empty village. 'Where all the people go?'

'They sailed away, Tingle.'

'Ran away,' Sherman says with a grunt, opening one eye.

'Can you blame them? The War Creatures are coming.'

'Meanie stinkers?' Tingle's ears flatten back against her head.

'They're not here yet, don't worry,' I tell her. Knowing she's relying on me to keep her safe makes me feel even worse.

'Tingle have yum yums now?'

'Er . . .'

See? I haven't even thought about food! How are we even supposed to survive on this stupid journey? I don't know. I've got no idea. We'll all starve if the War Creatures don't get us first!

'Tingle very hungry, Brat-Brat!'

Her desperate voice grates in my ear. There's no way I can do this. None. Lord Macawber should never have asked it of me. He knew how useless I am. And now we're all doomed.

'Here you go, tuck in.' Molly sits down next to us with a big bowl of kale and fish. I do my own impression of a codfish by staring at her and opening and closing my mouth over and over.

'Yay Molly! Tingle love fish yums.'

Tingle flicks fish into her mouth with a claw while Sherman snags the rich white chunks with his tongue.

'Molly? What are you doing here?' I ask, cramming the leftover kale in my mouth, just discovering how hungry I am.

'I'm getting everything ready for our mission,' she says.

'Our mission?'

'Yes. First we're going to Arberra to warn them and then we'll get into the Domed City and find a way to stop that army.'

'You mean you're coming with me?'

'Of course I am!' Molly says. 'I saw those monsters, didn't I? Warning people of what's coming is important.'

I resist the urge to throw my arms around her. Molly isn't useless like me. She's brave and strong. She knows how to survive out here. With her help we might just manage it.

'Besides,' she adds with a wide grin. 'I'm not letting you have all the fun.'

'Fun?'

'Yes of course! Travel, adventure . . .'

'Danger, risk, being chased by giant ravenous monsters . . .' I add.

'Well, it's still more fun than staying here!' she insists, and I decide not to argue. I don't want to put her off coming.

'But how will we even get into the Domed

City?' I grab another handful of food before it disappears into Tingle and Sherman. 'Cassy said it was impossible.'

'Aye, well, my ma doesn't know everything.'

'Your ma?'

Molly nods. 'Total pain having your ma being the leader but just sometimes it works in my favour. She was so busy worrying about everyone else she didn't even notice when I jumped off the boat.'

'She's going to be furious when she finds out!' I say, thinking how nice it must be to have someone who cares.

'Aye, but she can't risk everyone else by coming back for me so . . .' Molly shrugs.

'Do you really think we can make it?' I ask her. Cassy and Kendrick had been so adamant it was impossible, a worm of doubt is eating at my belly.

'I think we can try. And I'd rather die trying than live wondering what might have happened if I hadn't tried, wouldn't you?' Her eyes are dancing with excitement at the danger ahead. 'Anyway, we can't stay here, can we?'

'No,' I agree. 'We can't do that.'

'So . . . let's get moving then. I'd rather not die just because you're too lazy to shift your bum!'

Molly strides ahead, a long spear clutched in one hand, Tingle sitting on her shoulder chattering in her ear like they're best friends.

I follow behind pushing the wheelbarrow Molly dragged from a small shelter crowded with odds and ends. Maybe it's my destiny to push wheelbarrows?

This one is full of all the supplies Molly managed to sneak out of the boats. Enough to last us the long day's journey across the wastes and to offer up something to the Arberrans.

Oh and Sherman's in there too. We've only been walking for ten minutes when we realize we'll all be eaten by monsters if we keep to Sherman's pace so now I'm pushing him too.

At least I'm good at pushing wheelbarrows. And this one hasn't got a wobbly wheel. And I'm out in the fresh air instead of a mouldering old castle.

It's not pretty though. No trees, no grass,

no flowers, nothing. It's just endless cracked dry earth.

'What made them do it?' I ask Molly after a while. 'Why would the mages scorch the earth like this?'

Molly slows down and walks next to me. 'It's awful, isn't it? I forgot you haven't seen it before.'

'My master said it was a wasteland but I never imagined it was this bad!'

'The first mages used their skills to help people,' Molly says. 'They enhanced fields with magic so we'd have enough food, changed the weather to make sure crops would grow, healed sickness and disease.'

'So what happened?'

'The Magestreki happened. They were a group of mages who believed they were superior to normal folk and should rule over them like gods. The other mages disagreed, felt that their gift was given to them so they could work with and protect folk.'

'So they went to war then?'

'Yes. Each side became more and more desperate as it went on. the Magestreki were determined to win whatever the cost and didn't care about the damage they did to the earth or the people. Thousands died in the storms, earthquakes, and fires they unleashed. Thousands more in the plague, drought, and famine that came after.'

'Magestreki very bad!' Tingle says from her perch on Molly's shoulder.

'That's not even the worst of it, Tingle. Near the end, when they were close to losing, a few of the Magestreki used necromancy to bring the dead bodies back to life! The other side knew things had gone too far. They made plans to end the war once and for all. After building the Domed City for the few survivors and filling it with supplies, they joined their magic and sent out a spell that finally destroyed the Magestreki. But they sacrificed their own lives to do it.'

'Wow.' I try and imagine how hard it must have been, to give up their lives to save others.

'I know. Only five mages stayed behind and offered their services to the City but very few new mages were born after that. Lord Macawber was one of the last. I can't believe he never told you that story? All the children in the City are taught it in nursery.'

'He spent most of his time talking about getting his revenge on Lord Karush for banishing him, or how much he missed his daughter. I never knew the history before, not properly.'

'Well that history is why necromancy is forbidden, why he was banished from the City for attempting it.'

And yet he'd just carried on using it anyway, and I had stood by and watched like the fool I was.

'How do you all manage to live out here in the wastes?' I ask Molly, changing the subject quickly before I start to feel even worse. 'It must be impossible.'

'It is nearly. If it wasn't for the reef that surrounds us we'd all have died when they threw us out.'

'The reef?'

'During the earthquakes huge parts of Niyandi Mor fell away, they sank into the sea and created a reef. It traps the fish close to shore and every season we get a few enormous fish called leviathans washing up on the beach. They can't get back over the reef and when they die we use their flesh for food, their bones for shelter, their skin for leather, their fat for oil, their guts for rope . . . they keep us alive, basically.'

'That's lucky then.'

'I guess. Plus Ma managed to heal part of the land with this special compost she makes from seaweed and ash and fish bones. After years of trying we've got a small garden now and enough vegetables to keep us healthy.'

'Really? I didn't know anyone had managed to grow anything out here without magic!'

Molly shrugs. 'You never had to worry about it, did you? I bet you had everything you wanted with a mage to provide it.'

'No . . . Well, we had a magically enhanced garden so there were some vegetables and apples . . . and we had crab traps and eggs from the birds nesting on the cliffs. Oh and sometimes ships would come from the Southlands and bring supplies in return for my master's magic . . .' I stop talking, feeling guilty and ungrateful.

'That's what they have in the City,' Molly says. 'Magically enhanced gardens, acres of them. They even have a whole orchard and miles of strawberry bushes. I had one once. A strawberry, I mean. My pa brought it for me and it was the most amazing thing I've ever had. Rich and juicy and sweet . . .'

'Have you been in there then? In the City?'

'I was born there but Pa got cast out when I was five or so and Ma wouldn't stay without him. I don't really remember the place much so it will be good to see it again.'

'Do you really think we can get in, then?'

'Maybe.' She sniffs. 'I've got contacts.'

'I have to find Ellari. Lord Macawber's daughter. She can save us, he said.'

'Huh . . .'

'What?'

'Well, it's funny isn't it? Your master made all these monsters so he could save her and now she's got to save us from the monsters he made to save her!'

'It's not that funny.'

'No.' Molly sighs. 'It's not. I reckon we should just stop using magic altogether. It never does any good, does it?'

'What do you mean? What about strawberries?'

'Ah, but we wouldn't need magic to grow the strawberries if magic hadn't ruined the land in the first place, would we?'

I can't think of a reply so it goes quiet for a bit. Eventually Molly says we should stop for a rest and I drop the barrow gratefully and collapse on the hard earth.

Sherman clambers out and yawns.

'Tiring is it? Being pushed about in a barrow?' I ask.

'Tingle want to be pushed about in a barrow!' Tingle says, abandoning Molly and crawling into my lap for a cuddle.

'You're already being carried Tingle, I think that's enough, don't you?'

'Tingle need barrow. Tingle need nap. Tingle very tired.'

'How about I get in the barrow and you push me?' I suggest.

'No! Brat-Brat very good at pushing barrow.'

'Are you?' Molly drops down next to me

and hands me a skin of water.

'It's true. I am an expert. Years of training.' I take a long drink.

'Really? What were you doing in that castle all these years anyway?'

'Pushing a wheelbarrow mainly.'

Molly laughs. 'And?'

'And chopping up dead things to feed the monsters, clearing up dung, scrubbing out cages. Plus all the cooking and cleaning and mending, plus every other thing Lord Macawber might want.'

Molly raises an eyebrow at me. 'Fun then?'

'Barrels of it.' I huff out a breath.

'So why did you stay?'

I shrug. 'He saved my life when I washed up on the shore. I wouldn't even be here if it wasn't for him. I owed him.'

'Even though he was making a monster army?'

I can see that Molly thinks I was wrong to stay and she's right, of course she is, but it wasn't that easy.

I puff out my breath. 'I know it sounds stupid now but I never really thought he'd go through with it. I thought he'd get over his grief and anger one day and give it all up. I tried my best to get him to stop but he'd get furious whenever I suggested it and sometimes he'd throw things at me . . .'

'You should have just run away if he was that bad. Why didn't you just come to us?'

I squirm a little.

'My master said we wouldn't be welcome here.'

Molly's face is outraged. 'What a liar! We welcome everyone. Every outcast has a place with us if they want it. My ma offered you a place in the boat, didn't she?'

I lower my voice so my friends can't hear. 'Yes, but she also said Tingle and Sherman couldn't come. Said they couldn't be trusted because they were monsters, too.'

'What?' Molly flounders, her face pink. 'But . . . she told me you didn't want to come with us.'

I shrug. 'It doesn't matter. I couldn't have left anyway.'

'But . . . I can't believe she did that. I'm sorry, Brat.'

'It's not your fault. I don't blame them for being scared. I'm scared of lots of things . . . the sea terrifies me, the monsters petrify me . . . I'm just a big coward really.'

'I guess we're all afraid of something.' Molly says.

'Even you? I didn't think you were afraid of anything. You rescued us from the monsters, you beat them with your oar!'

She shakes her head, 'I didn't have a chance to be scared, that's all. I acted because I had to.'

'Well, I think you're brave, Molly.'

'Brave is doing something even when you're frightened,' Molly says, her brown eyes entirely honest. 'Like you staying in that castle even though you were scared all the time, and crossing the sea even though you were terrified, and now you're doing your best to warn everyone, despite the danger.'

I can feel my cheeks getting hot. I don't know what to say. I'm not used to people saying nice things.

Tingle helps by jumping down and declaring that, 'Tingle the most bravest though!' which makes me and Molly laugh.

'And Sherman the most grumpiest.'

'Tingle the stinkiest!' Sherman snaps back and the sound of them bickering is surprisingly soothing.

'We should eat something, keep our strength up.' Molly gets up and throws me a green biscuit from a basket in the barrow, giving me a wink when I catch it. 'We've got a long walk ahead of us and that wheelbarrow isn't going to push itself, is it?'

10

I feel better after I've eaten. Which is just as well because Molly sets off walking even faster than before and now I've got Sherman and Tingle sleeping in the barrow while I push it.

The sun keeps moving higher into the sky and no one is talking any more. Exhaustion has taken over. My arms and legs feel like they're going to drop off any minute and I'm mainly walking in a dazed stupor.

The barren landscape does little to distract me. A couple of hours ago we found a river and the slash of cool blue was inviting enough to send Tingle charging towards it.

Molly caught her mid-leap.

'You don't want to go in there, Tingle, it'll

burn your fur right off.'

Tingle mewed and buried her face in Molly's shoulder.

'How can the water burn?' I asked.

'All the water becomes fouled as it filters through the poisoned earth. We can't drink it or even use it for washing.'

'So where does your water come from?'

'We have a seawater converter. It's our most precious thing. Kendrick made it from spare parts, he makes one for each of the villages. Before that we had to filter our pee, and let me tell you, it wasn't much fun.'

I repressed a shudder. 'What does it do? The converter?'

'Takes the salt out of the water so we can drink it but it's slow and not very reliable so we have to ration it carefully. I've got enough water to last us the day and we can restock in Arberra tonight.'

'No swimming for you then, Tingle.'

'Tingle not like it out here,' she said crossly. 'It very bad place.'

The further we travel the more I agree with her. The river still runs to one side but it's far below us now. Our path has taken us up into a labyrinth of canyons, another gift from the Mage War and the earthquakes they caused.

There is some shade to be had here at least, where the high granite rocks block the sun, but the steep path has near finished me off.

When the wheelbarrow starts shaking and wobbling with Tingle and Sherman's fighting I give up entirely and set it down.

'Tingle biscuit!'

'Sherman biscuit!'

'Tingle biscuit!'

'Sherman biscuit!'

I wipe the sweat from my forehead and grab the water skin hanging from the handle. I take a few gulps of warm water, careful not to empty it now I know there's no easy way to replace it.

'Stop arguing about biscuits!' I snap. 'You're not supposed to be scoffing all the supplies.'

'But Tingle very hungry and Tingle like biscuits,' Tingle says.

'Sherman like biscuits, too.'

'Sherman very greedy.'

'No. Tingle greedy.'

'Not!'

I groan and collapse in the cool shadow of the tall rock behind me. Hours of pushing a wheelbarrow on no sleep and barely any food is taking its toll. What with fleeing for my life, nearly drowning, and almost being killed by monsters, I'm straying pretty close to my limits.

I know I can't stop here for long though. However much I may want to.

The monsters are coming. They'll have crossed the causeway at dawn so they can't be far behind us now and we're still a fair way from Arberra I think.

I take one more swig of water and heave myself back to my feet. Molly's out of sight already so I'll have to push hard to catch her up.

'Come on then, give me one of those biscuits,' I tell Tingle and Sherman.

They turn around and stare at me guiltily, crumbs clustered around their mouths.

'You haven't eaten them all, have you?' I spy the empty basket in the barrow and my belly rumbles in protest. 'That food is for everyone not just you two greedy guts! What about me? What about Molly? You're a rotten, selfish pair and I can't believe I've been pushing you both for hours!'

'Brat . . .' Sherman says, bobbing up and down.

'No, I don't want to hear it,' I snap. 'I've had enough.'

'But Brat-Brat!' Tingle shouts, her ears flat against her head.

'I said no, Tingle! I've had enough of you both!'

And then the War Creature they were trying to warn me about knocks me flying with a great furred arm.

I land on my back with a thud and just manage to raise my arms over my face as huge razor-sharp claws rake down at me. I scream as they slice open my skin. Pain jerks me out of my shock and I kick out with my clogs and catch the creature in his snarling pantheera face.

It dazes him, just for a second, and gives me enough time to try and wriggle away but I'm not quite fast enough and his sharp claws rip into my calf and drag me back towards him.

I dig my nails into the earth, scrabbling wildly for any purchase, but it's no good. The monster is going to eat me and I have no weapons and Molly is too far away and I'm going to die.

I twist around, my heart jumping in my chest when I see the massive creature looming over me, half pantheera, half wolf, with the spiked whip-like tail of a kerreky lizard. I remember that vicious face from the cages.

'You are mine now, meeeeat boy,' it hisses at me, 'I have waited loooong to try your sweeeeet fleeessssh.'

Its mouth opens wide, long shining fangs descend towards my neck . . .

'No eat my Brat-Brat!' Tingle screeches, flying at the creature's head, a snarling, biting, spitting bundle of fur and claws.

The monster rears back in shock and Sherman digs his teeth into my tunic collar, pulling me away.

The monster leaps about, batting at Tingle with its paws, trying to dislodge her but she sticks to him like a burr. Her sharp claws dig deeply into the beast's eyes until he howls with pain and then she jumps off.

I stagger to my feet, gripping my bleeding arm to my chest and trying not to faint from the pain in my leg.

The creature whirls and lashes out with his whip-like tail but Tingle jumps nimbly out of its path, almost as if she's enjoying herself.

'Tingle! Come here,' I shout, terrified the spiked tail will hit her if she carries on. Tingle obeys me for once, runs over, and claws her way up to my neck.

The monster roars with anger and stumbles after us. But it's half-blind now, his eyes clawed and bleeding, which only seems to make him more furious. He lashes out with his arms, reaching for us wildly, teeth gnashing.

'I WILL FIND YOU,' it yells, staggering around the canyon. 'I CAN STILL SMELL YOUR SWEEEEET FLESHHHH!'

Tingle lets out a squeak of terror and the creature lurches in our direction, like something from a nightmare. There's no way to escape the thing. Not while blood leaks from my wounds like an iron-rich scent trail.

I back away and the monster follows, nose in the air, tongue out. He doesn't notice Sherman sneaking his way around behind him.

I'm close to the edge of the canyon now. Behind me is a hundred-foot drop.

'Now!' Sherman shouts and I grit my teeth and dive to the left.

Sherman charges, head tucked down into his shoulders. He barrels into the creature with enough force to send the monster flying right over the cliff edge.

Tingle, Sherman, and I are all standing on the edge staring down when Molly arrives.

'What's going on? Why were you all screaming?' Molly demands, out of breath from running.

'Meanie stinker!' Tingle says.

'What? Where?' She spins her head round looking for the threat.

'Down there,' I tell her, pointing at the river below and the skeletal remains of the creature floating in it.

11

Molly makes me lie down and starts bandaging
my wounds with strips ripped from the bottom
of my tunic.

'There's no time,' I hiss through teeth
tightly clamped against the pain. 'They're
coming, Molly.'

'I'm nearly done,' she snaps, tying the ends
together. 'Now just wait there a second and
let me check.'

Tingle squirms round my neck seeking
comfort as Molly runs back the way we came
and stands on the top of the slope looking
down. I know she's seen them when her back
stiffens, and when she turns around again her
face is bone-white.

'We have to go,' she says. 'Now.'

'How far away are they?' I ask as she helps pull me to my feet.

'Not far enough.'

'And how far are we from Arberra?'

'Half an hour maybe? If we hurry.'

'They'll catch us up, Molly—we won't even have time to warn them.' Panic is building in my chest.

'It's all right. I've got a plan. Just trust me.'

She slips her spear into the loops on the back of her tunic, heaves Sherman into the wheelbarrow, grabs the handles, and starts pushing. I limp behind her, sharp pain throbbing in my arm and leg with every step but I don't stop. I can't stop.

The War Creatures are coming.

/ \ / \ / \ \ / / / / \ / \ \ \ /

'Not far now!' Molly says, panting from the effort of pushing Sherman in the barrow. If I had any breath of my own I would tell her how grateful I am that she never once suggested leaving my friends behind. Or me for that matter. But I don't. So I can't.

I focus everything I have on forward motion.

We can hear them coming now. Faint roars and the dull, relentless thump of marching footsteps. Which means they're catching up. Which, despite being terrible news, is good for our motivation at least.

Molly stops at last and lowers the barrow. 'Arberra is just ahead, through that canyon.'

I look where she's pointing, at the narrow gap that runs between the huge granite mountains that fill the east horizon, continuing for miles in either direction.

'If they catch up with us there's nowhere to hide,' I tell her.

'Then we better make sure they don't catch up. Come on!'

She heaves the barrow up and starts running. Tingle dashes behind her and I find some spark of energy from somewhere and break in to an awkward trot.

'But Molly, what happens when we get to the end?'

'I've got a plan, trust me!'

What choice do I have? The canyon is cool at least, shadowed by the giant walls, but it seems never-ending. Pain jolts down my arm and leg with every step and my breath rasps in my throat.

'Hurry, Brat-Brat!' Tingle shouts from the far end. 'Meanie stinkers!'

Molly swears and increases her speed, pushing the barrow as fast as she can till she hits a bump and Sherman's tipped out onto his back. He flails around on his shell, his small legs waving helplessly in the air. Molly tries to heave him up but he's too heavy for her.

I make my legs go faster. When I reach them we lift Sherman back into the barrow together and stagger the last few feet to the end of the canyon.

I collapse with Sherman, feeling dizzy and sick, but Molly grabs her spear and starts hacking at a rope on the side of the canyon.

The roar of the monsters grows louder as they barge their way into the narrow gap. They can only come at us in single file but still they come . . . eyes burning with hunger.

'Molly! Whatever it is you're doing, you'd better do it now!'

'I'm trying!' she cries. 'My spear isn't sharp enough!'

I look at Tingle. She runs to help Molly, claws unsheathed.

I scramble backwards like a crab onto the rocky plain beyond, dragging Sherman with me, a scream locked in my throat as the monstrous horde of creatures, with their rabid teeth and claws, talons and tails, grows ever nearer.

And then there's a twang, followed by an almighty rumble, and half the canyon wall collapses, blocking the exit with huge slabs of stone and rubble and building an insurmountable wall between us and the ravenous monsters.

12

When the ruins of Arberra come into sight just as dusk falls, I'm almost ready to cry.

We'd escaped the monsters, just, slowed them down even, with Molly's clever plan of releasing the supports put in years ago when the canyon walls first started to crumble. But there is another way round, she said. It will take them time to get here but there's no doubt they will.

And now this broken, crumbling, yellow stone ruin, half buried in the sun-baked earth, offers up some small refuge at least.

'Where is everyone?' I whisper when we finally get inside the broken walls.

There is a hush around the place as if it's been deserted for a thousand years.

'They'll be at Jack's Place,' Molly tells me.

'Who's Jack?' I ask.

'No one. . . it's just the name of the tavern everyone goes to. Come on, follow me,' Molly says, dumping the barrow and helping to lift Sherman out. 'It's not far.'

Despite the long, terrible journey, Molly has a wild excitement burning in her eyes as she leads us through a cracked doorway and down a series of long tunnels, taking us deeper underground.

'Here we are!' Molly says, pushing the curtain away from the doorway and gesturing us inside.

A burst of noise followed by the sharp fumes of sweat and strong alcohol doesn't make me keen to enter but I'm too tired to argue.

Molly pushes me down on a chair at a round table.

'Wait here, I'll be back in a second.'

I watch Molly weave through the crowd of men and women who drink and shout and smoke, resting my sore arm on the table. The pain has got worse and worse, as if a worm is burrowing inside my skin, and my whole arm feels puffy and hot. It's blocking out the pain from my leg, though, so that's something at least.

'Tingle not like it here,' she says, crawling onto my lap and hiding in my tunic.

Sherman tucks himself under my feet with a grunt. No one's looking at either of them though. They're too busy drinking and gambling and fighting.

'We won't be staying long,' I tell them, which is a shame because now I've sat down I'm not sure I can ever get up again.

I almost drop my head on the table to have a quick nap but then I hear Molly's name being shouted.

I spy her curly head at the back of the room. She's standing by a table of men.

'All right, Pa?' I hear her say and a tall, burly man with red hair pulls her into a hug.

'All right?' he says. 'I'm better than all right seeing my own little flower! What are you doing here? You haven't crossed the wastes on your own, have you? I told you it's not safe.'

'No, I came with a friend.' She starts pulling him across the room towards us.

'Any particular reason? You're not in trouble, are you?'

'No . . .' Molly says. 'Well, yes we are in trouble but first can we help Brat? He's been hurt.'

'I'm fine,' I say, standing up when they approach. Only instead of standing up I fall over.

Molly's dad catches me and hoists me up into his arms.

'All right, lad,' he says. 'We'll get you sorted, don't you worry. You're safe now.'

I want to tell him that I'm not safe, none of us are safe, the War Creatures are coming, but instead I decide it's best to pass out.

13

Wet sandpaper scrapes at my eyelids. I wrench them open and find Tingle's bright-green eyes peering into mine.

'Yay! Brat not dead,' she says.

'Not quite.' I manage a smile and she carries on licking my face. I reach a hand down to stroke Sherman, who's lying on the floor next to me, and he lets out a soft grunt of pleasure as my fingers scratch under his shell and round his stitches.

I'm lying on a small couch in a dingy room. I struggle to sit up, still feeling groggy and sore but the pain in my arm and leg has eased. They're now encased in bandages that smell faintly of the sea.

Molly appears at my side and helps me get

upright.

'What happened?'

'You passed out. It was just as well, Irina said. She had to clean out your wounds with alcohol before sewing them up.'

I swallow down the bile that rises in my throat at the thought.

'I'm glad I missed it.'

'She's wrapped them in a seaweed poultice and said they should heal well if you're careful.'

'Where are we? How long was I out?'

'We're still at Jack's, just out the back in the staffroom. You've only been out an hour or so.' She hands me a clay cup. 'Drink that. It's to stop infection, Irina said.'

I take a sip and make a face at the sour taste. I down it one go though because I've just remembered why we're here.

'We need to leave,' I say, getting awkwardly to my feet. 'Have you warned them?'

'My dad's doing it now. He's talking to Patches.'

I peer over where her finger points and see Molly's dad sitting at a corner table with a large, dark-haired man in a patched waistcoat.

'You didn't tell me your pa lived here. I guess he's why you were so keen to come?'

'Well, I couldn't just leave him to die, could I? Even if Ma could . . .' Her voice fades away.

'They don't live together any more then?' I ask.

Molly shakes her head. 'Not for years. They tried but Pa couldn't bear it at the village and Ma couldn't bear it at Arberra and I didn't get any choice in any of it.'

'So what does he do here anyway?'

'He's a smuggler,' she says proudly. 'One of the best there is. He trades with his contact in the City for the things that help us survive. Some people say he's a traitor for dealing with the City but they're happy to take all the supplies he gets.'

'So, your pa knows a way into the City then? A secret way?'

'Yep, he's going to take us later.'

I feel a bit easier knowing we have a way in but I wish there was some sign of action. They have to evacuate the town, get to the coast and out of the path of the monsters or the carnage will be terrible to behold.

'I can't believe we made it,' Molly says, sitting down next to me.

'We almost didn't,' I say. 'We wouldn't have if it wasn't for you.'

'I was just lucky Pa told me about the repairs to the canyon.'

'Lucky Tingle has special, sharp claws!' she says.

Luck on our side again then? I wonder how much more we have left. And if it's going to be enough for what we still have to do.

Molly brings me a bowl of soup and some bread and I wolf it down, pushing Tingle's questing head away because I know they've already been fed.

'My daughter wouldn't lie!' The angry voice floats across the room. 'If she says she's seen them then she has!'

There's a loud snort. 'A monster army? How drunk are you exactly, Connor?'

A burst of laughter.

Molly and I peer over at the corner.

'I'm not drunk!' Connor gets to his feet and points his finger at Patches. 'You have to listen, people are in danger.'

'I don't have to listen to poxy fairy tales your crazy daughter dreamt up!'

'Come on, Brat,' Molly says, her face furious. 'We'll tell him.'

'All right.' I get carefully to my feet.

'And you two better come too,' she says to Tingle and Sherman. 'You can prove what Lord Macawber was up to all these years!'

I limp after Molly as she barges over to the table where Patches sits. Two big men with biceps as big as my head stand behind Patches looking menacing but they don't seem to bother Molly at all.

'I'm no liar, Patches, and my dad's no drunk!' she insists. 'There's an army of monsters coming and I can prove it to you!'

She waves a hand at Tingle and Sherman.

Patches scratches his dark beard with a lazy finger. 'Monsters? Them?' He points at Tingle and Sherman. 'I reckon we can cope with a few of those little freaks easy enough . . .'

Sherman's head retreats inside his shell but Tingle puffs up with anger.

'Tingle not freak!' she says, her voice rising high with indignation. 'Stupid, stinky bum-face man.'

Patch jerks back in surprise when he hears her speak and a slight frown crosses his face.

'They're not what you have to worry about anyway! They were the first ones he made,' Molly insists. 'The ones coming are worse. Much worse. Brat knows, he was there when they were made, he looked after them. He's the expert!'

Patches looks me up and down, his lip curling.

'Expert is he? Not an expert at locking cages though is he, if all these "monsters" of his have escaped? Come on then "expert", tell me all about them.'

Suddenly it feels like I'm back in the castle with Lord Macawber telling me I'm useless and no good. I can feel my throat close.

'They're very dangerous . . .' I mutter.

Patch snorts loudly.

Molly frowns at me and I can feel myself shrivel with shame.

'I've seen them myself, Patch! A hundred or more. Great beasts with giant claws and teeth,' Molly says. 'I slowed them down but they're marching this way now. We've got no chance against them. None. You have to evacuate!'

'We've been banished from our home once. We're not leaving again,' he tells her, swigging his beer.

'Look,' she says. 'If you want to stay here and die it's up to you but don't you think the people here have a right to know what's coming so they can make their own choice?'

'I'm the leader here,' he says, lifting his chin. 'They follow my rules.'

'You're not a leader,' Molly spits. 'You're a stubborn old fool.'

She climbs up on a chair and stamps her foot for attention. 'LISTEN! There's an army of monsters heading this way. They'll kill you all if they get the chance. Leave now while you still can!'

The tavern erupts into chaos with people demanding to know what's going on and when the monsters are coming. Patches tries to keep control but pretty soon fists are flying and cups are smashed as the residents demand answers. None of them notice when we're grabbed by Patches' two big henchmen and hauled away by the hair.

14

We're dumped in a cold, dark cell and the heavy wooden door clangs shut behind us.

I untie the wriggling sack at my feet and let Tingle and Sherman out.

'Tingle no like sack!' she says, licking furiously at her mussed up fur.

Sherman looks slowly around our new home and sighs loudly. 'Not much better out here.'

He's right. It is a miserable place. The stone walls are dripping with water and black mould creeps across the ceiling. There are two wooden buckets in the corner but no bed and no blanket, just a scattering of rags to cover the floor.

'I can't believe Patches is locking us up in

this fleapit instead of doing something useful!' Molly fumes.

'I should have known he wouldn't listen in the first place,' Connor says, shaking his head.

'It's not your fault,' I tell him. 'You tried your best, so did Molly.'

Guilt writhes in my gut again. Maybe I could have convinced him if I'd tried. If I wasn't so scared and useless. Now we're locked up and there's no chance of getting to the City. No chance of stopping the monsters. No chance of putting my mistakes right.

'Tingle no like it here, Brat-Brat!' she says loudly, her nose wrinkling at the smell of damp and pee that fills the chill air.

'I know. I'm sorry.' I scoop her up and give her a cuddle, finding some comfort in her warm fur and soft purring.

My arm and leg are throbbing again after being practically dragged down two streets and some steps by Patches' burly goons but the pain of my failure hurts far worse.

Molly pounds at the door with her fists, peering through the small barred window.

'Let us out!' she shouts. 'We didn't do

anything!'

It hasn't escaped my notice that for once I am on the other side of the cell door and I don't much like it.

Molly puffs out her cheeks and blows all the air out noisily when her efforts bring no result. 'What are we going to do now?'

'Come and sit with your old pa. We'll think of something, don't worry.'

Molly thumps herself down next to Connor and he wraps one arm around her shoulders. 'Why wouldn't he believe us though, Pa? Why would we lie?'

'Ah, Patch don't trust anyone. He thinks he's some sort of king and we're all trying to steal his stupid crown.'

'Tingle like crown!' she says, perking up slightly.

'Get us out of here and I'll make you one myself,' Molly tells her.

'Yay!' Tingle says before going strangely quiet.

'I can't believe he'd really risk everyone like this,' I say, thinking about all the people I've seen today in Arberra.

'Plenty of people heard what we told them,' Molly says.

'Aye, I reckon there'll be a fair few sneaking away when they get the chance. Patches might find it's just him and his goons by the time those monsters arrive!'

'And us,' Sherman reminds him.

We all look at the locked door and go quiet. We aren't going anywhere at the moment, that's for sure.

15

Molly is full of nervous energy. She fidgets and paces and whistles and hums.

I sit quietly in the corner, turning Lord Macawber's golden locket over and over in my hands.

'What's that?' Molly asks when she spies it.

'This is what was going to save us. Ellari could have used it to drain the magic from the creatures.'

'Only Ellari can use it?'

'She's the only one with the magic who can activate it.'

'How does she activate it then?'

I shrug. 'I don't know anything about magic really. Ellari would know though, wouldn't she?'

Molly frowns. 'So if she could somehow magically activate the locket, all the creatures Macawber made would what . . . fall over and die?'

'I think so. The monsters can't live without the magic inside them, can they?'

A heavy thud of dread echoes in my heart as the reality of what I've just said sinks in.

I glance at Tingle and Sherman arguing quietly in the corner and my belly turns over. Bitter bile rises in my throat and I throw myself at the bucket just in time.

'Sorry,' I mutter afterwards, wiping my face with my sleeve.

'Don't be silly. It's not your fault,' Molly says. 'This place is enough to make anyone sick.'

I lie on the floor, feeling cold and shaky. What an idiot I am. How did I not realize before? If Ellari uses the locket to drain the magic from the monsters I'd have to sacrifice . . .

Everything.

I'm distracted by a sudden scrape of a key in the lock. The door opens a fraction and a small, hairy man in a filthy apron shoves a tray through the gap.

'Here,' he says. 'Grub's up.'

'Gruel is it? Lucky us,' Connor says.

'Lucky I didn't spit in it,' the jailer says with a leer.

'You should let us out, you know,' Molly tells him. 'There's a monster army coming. It's not right to keep us locked up.'

The man laughs till his belly shakes. 'That's a good one! A monster army. Haven't heard that one before.'

'It's true, you horrid, stinky old man!' Molly says.

The jailer frowns and glares at Molly. His hand reaches for the heavy iron rod strapped to his belt but Connor stands up and moves in front of his daughter, his eyes full of warning.

Could he fight him? Get the ring of keys hanging from his belt maybe?

But before Connor has the chance to try anything the jailer seems to realize the threat, sniffs, and slams the door shut. His little red face appears in the grate.

'I may be stinky, but least I'm not in jail, missy!' he says gleefully, locking the door as loudly as possible.

'Well, you should be!' Molly shouts back. 'For crimes against my nose!'

'I should have decked the little weasel,' Connor says.

'No, I should have!' Molly says and the two of them snort and then laugh.

I look at the offering of thin, white gruel on the tray. It looks a little like a sick slug sneezed into the clay bowls, and does nothing for my still-griping belly.

I look over at my friends, expecting Tingle to start complaining, but Tingle isn't there— which is impossible seeing as the room is tiny, there's nowhere to hide, and the door is locked.

'Tingle?' I call. 'Tingle! Where's Tingle, Sherman?'

Sherman shakes his head.

'TINGLE!' I shout. 'Where is she?' I grab Molly. 'Have you seen her?'

'Well . . . she can't have gone far, can she?'

'Then where is she? Suddenly turned invisible?' I don't understand. My eyes search the room frantically.

'She didn't go out when he opened the door, did she?' Connor asks.

I remember the open door behind the jailer, the small, Tingle-sized gap. 'No! She wouldn't just leave us.'

'Are you sure?'

'Yes! She's my friend! She wouldn't go anywhere!' I can feel my throat closing.

'But Brat . . . she must have,' Molly says, resting her hand on my shoulder.

'No.' I can't breathe. 'No.'

The pain of her loss stabs at me but . . . maybe this was her chance? If Tingle gets far enough away maybe she'll be safe? From the monsters. From the locket . . .

'Hello, Brat-Brat!'

I spin round and see Tingle's face peering in through the small grate in the door.

'Tingle! What are you doing out there?' I grab at her paws, stroke her face, reassure myself that she's really here.

'Tingle want out!' she says.

'Yes, but now you're out there and we're in here!'

'Brat come out too!'

'The door is locked, Tingle!' I shout in frustration.

'Brat-Brat use key!' she says, and her long tail dangles the jailer's ring of keys through the bars.

'Tingle! Did you steal his keys?' Molly asks, grabbing them from her tail. 'You little genius!'

'Yes. Tingle very clever! Tingle have crown now?'

'What?' Molly asks, reaching her arm through the bars and inserting the first key in the lock.

'Molly says she make Tingle crown when we get out!'

The door swings open and I scoop Tingle into my arms and squeeze her till she squeaks.

'Ouchie Brat-Brat!'

'Serves you right for scaring me!' I snap, loosening my hold just a smidge.

'But Tingle be very clever!'

'Yes, but it might have been more clever if you'd told me. I thought you'd gone . . .'

Tingle cocks her head to one side and looks at me. 'Gone? Where Tingle go without Brat-

Brat?'

'Nowhere! Tingle goes nowhere without me, got it?' Despite my happiness at her return, a faint pang of regret fills me. Her fate is tied up with mine now.

Tingle nods and licks my nose.

'Er, do you actually want to leave then or what?' Molly demands.

So many thoughts rush through my brain. This is it then. Because of Tingle we have a chance again, a chance to get to the City and give the locket to Ellari and save everyone. I have to do it, don't I? Save everyone, whatever it might cost me?

I hurry out of the cell towards Molly. If I don't do anything then we're all dead anyway.

Connor moves between me and Molly and puts one arm around each of us. 'You lot are the best jail mates I've ever had,' he says. 'And definitely the most useful.'

'Then get us out of here, Pa, before that horrid man realizes we've gone.'

'I can do that, Mollykins,' he says.

We follow Connor down a few dark and dank corridors and out through a back door cut in the wall.

The low sunlight is enough to make me squint when we step outside but the rush of fresh air is worth it. We are free.

But that one second of joy is split by an enormous roaring that hurts my ears, swiftly followed by the heavy thunderous footsteps of an army descending on Arberra like a tidal wave of death.

16

'They're here.' My voice sounds hollow.

In the distance I can see the ranks of monsters destroying the town walls and smashing their way through the ruins.

Molly stares at them with wide eyes, frozen to the spot.

Tingle curls herself around my neck, trembling from head to toe.

Sherman rolls his eyes as if to say, of course they're here, you fool.

And Connor turns white and pasty as the reality of my words sinks in.

'Take us to the City,' I snap at him, surprising myself with the strength in my voice, forcing him to action before it's too late. 'Now, Connor!'

He nods, glad of something to focus on, and starts running through the ruined town. I grab Molly's arm and pull her along with me.

The people of Arberra, the few who haven't already left, start running out of their houses and filling the streets with their panic. Some of them have weapons, crossbows, and swords that they try and use against their enemy.

They're easily picked off by the War Creatures.

Trampled, snatched, devoured. Their weapons crushed beneath their feet.

I keep my eyes fixed on Connor and try not to think about the death surrounding us. Try not to listen to the screaming and wailing and vicious laughter filling the dusk.

Connor pauses behind a wall, avoiding the giant half-bear, half-ogre creature rampaging across the way.

Sherman catches us up, his breathing hoarse and troubled.

'How far is it, Connor?' I whisper. 'Sherman's struggling.'

He points just beyond the town walls at a well house a hundred yards or so away. 'Don't worry lad, I'll take him.'

I nod my thanks. We can make it. If there's enough of a gap we can make it. We have to.

Molly is crouching on the ground, her arms over her head, her whole body shaking.

'Molly, it's not far now. Just hold on,' I tell her, though it feels strange to be the brave one for a change.

'I didn't know,' she says, her voice coming in short, sharp gasps. 'I thought I knew, I saw the others, I thought I understood about the army when you told me but . . . I didn't.'

Before I can answer, the wall behind us crumbles. A giant bull-headed creature with the body of a lionus bursts through and we dive out of the way, just missing being trampled.

'RUN!' I shout at Connor, taking Molly's hand and dragging her behind me.

Connor swallows, hauls Sherman into his arms, and plunges into the mayhem. I avoid the slash of eagle claws, duck under a lashing lizard tail, and follow him as best I can while keeping hold of Molly.

'DESTROY THEM ALL!' The maddened

battle cry of their leader echoes across the ruined town. 'FLEE FOOLISH MORTALS BUT YOU CANNOT ESCAPE DEATH!'

I turn my head and see Wrath striding through the broken bodies, his huge arms lashing out, smashing walls and felling two large men waving clubs as easily as if they were rag dolls.

They're the same ones who dragged us off to jail but I feel no pleasure at their suffering. My heart races in my chest as I watch, memories of Lord Macawber's screams fill my head, and I almost fall.

'Brat!' Molly shouts, pulling on my hand. 'We have to go, please!'

I swallow down my terror and start moving. I can just see Connor at the edge of town. It's not far. We can do this. We can make it.

Can't we?

Together the three of us scramble our way through the confusion to where Sherman and Connor are waiting for us. Connor pulls a terrified Molly into his arms and squeezes her tight.

'Nearly there, my flower. Don't you worry.'

I reach up and give Tingle a quick stroke.

'Tingle no like meanie stinkers,' she whispers in my ear. 'Tingle 'fraid.'

'We're going to be fine,' I tell her, squashing down my own terror. We have to be. I won't let my mistakes rob Molly and Connor and all the other good people of their lives. 'It will all be over soon.'

'One way or another,' Sherman predicts grimly under his breath.

I ignore him and focus on the gap between us and safety. Twenty yards maybe, and reasonably clear of trouble compared to the rest of the town.

'Let me go first,' Connor says in a hushed voice. 'Then come quickly and quietly, we don't want those things to try and follow us.'

I nod and watch him dash, as well as anyone can dash when they're half crouched over, carrying a heavy Sherman and trying not to be spotted by the vicious monsters all around, over to the well house.

It's not particularly sturdy-looking. Just a rough stone shelter that covers the well and keeps it out of the heat. A pile of leather buckets are piled up around it and I imagine someone has the thankless job of using them to fill up the troughs in town a few times a day. It might not look like much but right now it is the promised land. Offering sanctuary from the carnage, the final step towards our goal and the only chance at salvation.

Connor reaches the well house, ducks inside, and waves us to follow. Molly takes a deep breath, squares her shoulders and runs. I hurry after her, keeping my eye out for creatures and trying not to wince as the stitches in my leg come loose and blood starts seeping from the wound.

Deep inside the well house I can see Connor working to open the heavy metal hatch in the ground, his muscles straining sharply to lift it.

With a mighty heave, the hatch finally opens but Connor loses his grip and it slips from his fingers and falls backwards with a loud clang.

Molly freezes.

Did they hear? I swivel my head round but the creatures are busy with their slaughter and so I push Molly to get her moving again.

She gulps down her fear and sprints the final few yards.

I'm close behind, desperate to be out of sight of the monsters. I turn around to check we haven't been spotted and my eyes are caught by a figure running towards us.

I squint and make out the patches on his coat . . .

'WAIT!' he yells, terror claiming his common sense entirely. 'Connor! Wait for me!'

I swear under my breath and slide into the shelter.

'What is that fool doing? He's going to get us all killed,' Connor hisses.

'Quickly then, before they see us!'

Connor helps Molly into the hatch and she starts climbing down the metal rungs. I pick Tingle off my neck and she scampers down after her easily enough.

Sherman waddles his way to the hatch and I frown. He'll never get down those steps.

'WAIT FOR ME!' Patches bellows again.

I spin my head to see the terror stricken leader barrelling towards us but I'm not the only one to notice him.

A nightmarish arachnoid monster, with an eight-legged tarantula body, the mawed head of a giant flesh-eating leech, and the long serrated tail of a sea scorpion follows Patches with his many eyes.

'You go now,' Connor says to me, his eyes on the monster. 'I can carry Sherman.'

The creature starts moving towards Patches, its twelve beady black eyes fixed on his fleeing body.

There's no time to argue, so I drop down the hole and start climbing.

Connor swiftly follows. He's tucked Sherman close to his chest inside his shirt, leaving his arms free to hold the ladder while the other shuts the hatch.

I look down and see Molly and Tingle waiting for us on a wooden platform a few feet below. They've lit a small lantern and when the hatch clangs shut it stops us from being entirely in the dark.

When I look up again Connor isn't moving. He's trying desperately to hold the hatch in place but it's jerked out of his hands.

The faint lantern light illuminates Patches' horrified face.

'HELP ME!' he screams but it's too late, the creature's sharp serrated tail wraps around him and tries to pull him back.

Patches screams as he tries to pull himself away, overbalances and falls, dragging the creature down after him.

The hatch slams shut.

Man and monster plummet past Connor and then me as we cling to the ladder, before hitting the platform below, destroying the lantern, and plunging us all into sudden, haunting darkness.

The sound of them crashing right through the wood and hitting the water below follows swiftly.

The deep, dark blackness of the well swallows me up and my breath comes in shallow bursts as I wonder what happened to Molly and Tingle below.

17

'Brat-Brat?' Tingle's voice breaks the long, tense silence.

'Sssshhh!' Molly hisses and I gasp with pent-up relief. They're alive!

'It's all right,' Connor calls back. 'We can't wait here in silence all night. Is everyone OK?'

'No, Tingle no like the dark!'

'Good point, Tingle. We'll get that sorted in a minute. Molly my love, how's the platform?' Connor asks.

'Smashed and wobbly. They only just missed landing on me and Tingle.'

'But you haven't heard or seen anything move?'

'No.'

'We can't assume that monster's dead, can

we?' Connor asks.

'Well, it did fall very hard and they're not very good in water so it might be,' I tell him.

'Just to be on the safe side, can you throw something in, Molly, see if it moves at all?'

'All right, hang on.' After a minute of groping around in the dark, Molly must find a stone or something. There's a plop in the water and we all hold our breath waiting for a sign . . .

'I think that's the best we can hope for. The impact or the water must have killed them,' says Connor after a minute or so of silence. 'Poor old Patches. He might have been an idiot but no one deserves a grisly death like that. . .'

'At least we're still alive.' Molly says.

'That's true, my lovely, and there's no time for moping. Brat?'

'Yes,' I reply through clamped-together teeth. The pain in my arm and leg is getting hard to bear, and clinging to a metal rung in the cold and dark isn't helping much. 'If you keep climbing down past the platform, you'll come to a rope tied to the rail. Follow that rope and you'll find the boat. On the boat there are candles.'

'All right.' I start climbing slowly and carefully, wary of slipping and falling and joining Patches and that hideous War Creature at the bottom of the water.

I find the rope and the boat bobbing nearby. It takes me an age to climb into it. Partly because I can't see and my leg is wobbly, and partly because my fear of water has not miraculously disappeared after my headlong dash across the causeway.

When I'm finally in the boat and sitting down at last I let out a huge sigh of relief. But the darkness is breathing down my neck and despite the still water I have to try hard not to imagine the arachnoid monster reaching out of the water and dragging me down with him into the black depths.

I focus instead on trying to find and light a candle in the dark.

Eventually my numb fingers get a spark from the flint and there is light again. A small glow that nonetheless makes everything feel better.

'Yay, Brat-Brat!' Tingle shouts. 'Tingle like

light!'

I can see the two of them standing on a small square of splintered wood and send thanks to the spirits that they hadn't been crushed.

Connor climbs down the last part of the ladder and steps into the boat beside me with a relieved grin. He releases Sherman and sets him down in the bottom.

'He's heavier than he looks, isn't he?' Connor says.

Sherman grunts and retreats from the indignity of it all by hiding inside his oversized shell.

Connor unties the rope from the rail, grabs the oars, and moves the boat easily around the broken platform to collect Molly and Tingle.

Tingle leaps into my arms and I spill wax on my hand but the pain is worth it to have her furry little body snuggled close to me.

Molly hugs her pa and lets out a shaky sigh.

'That was horrible,' she says. 'You were so brave though, Brat. I wouldn't have made it without you.'

My cheeks grow hot at her words but I can't help smiling a little. Maybe I'm not such a coward after all?

'I can't believe those monsters killed everyone . . .' she adds, her small body still shuddering.

'Not everyone,' Connor reminds her. 'Lots of people escaped, Molly, and that was thanks to you two. But you were right about the danger, Brat. The City must be warned.'

'But how do we get there from here?' I ask, gazing around the small enclosed lake.

Connor grins. 'That, my friend, is the best-kept secret in all Niyandi Mor.'

18

Connor pulls back the oars and rows to the far edge of the small lake. We slip through a concealed gap in the rock wall and slide down a small waterfall onto an actual underground river.

I blow out the candle. We don't need it here because the walls are shining with some sort of glowing moss. It is easy to see the canyon surrounding us, vast acres of yellow rock smoothed by thousands of years of water rushing through it.

'It's the only way the City and Arberra can survive. The water for this river comes from deep underground and doesn't pick up the poison from the earth. It feeds our well and the City, and this is how we smuggle goods back and forth.'

'It's amazing, Pa!' Molly says.

'And fast. Instead of half a day of hard walking we'll be there in an hour or so.'

'How did you find it?'

'Luck mainly. When I lived in the City my job was maintaining the water pipes. I got drunk one day when I was fixing a pipe and fell in. I got washed down to that lake, climbed up, and found the ruins of Arberra. When I jumped back in it took me ages to find the gap but I knew it had to be there so I just kept looking. When I found it at last, I swam my way back to the City.'

The horrors above seem very far away down here and I can feel the tension leaving my body as Connor rows the small boat forward.

'Years later when that cranking great toerag Karush threw me out for gambling, I joined Patches in Arberra and started trading with my contact in the City. Patches was desperate to know my secret but I never told him, even when I was drunk, even when he locked me up!'

'You never told me either!' Molly says.

'It's not a secret if you tell people, is it?'

'But I'm your daughter!'

'I haven't forgotten. It was best you didn't know, that way no one could force you to tell.'

'Who would force me to tell?'

He shrugs.

'Ma? Did you think Ma would try and force me?'

'No, not really . . . but she hates what I do.'

'She hates that you're away all the time and doing something dangerous . . . so do I.' Molly adds the last part under her breath.

'What would happen if you got caught?' I ask, saving Connor from having to reply.

He sighs. 'Karush would have me killed I reckon. And the people who trade with me, too.'

'Wow. That's a bit extreme, isn't it?'

'Karush runs that place like a prison. Every year his rule gets stricter and stricter. Any sign of rebellion and they're out. No one can vote against him for fear they and their families will end up being cast out of the City.'

'What is it you smuggle anyway?'

'There isn't much we have that they need but they'll pay for the spirits we make at Arberra and the leviathan oil from the villages.'

'Pay with what?'

'Anything. Tools, equipment, tins and jars, dry food, meat occasionally, candles . . . the outcasts need it all.'

'How does the City have so much stuff? I know they have magically enhanced fields and things but where do all their other supplies come from?'

'The mages left a huge stockpile of goods beneath the City. Supposed to last them long enough to heal the land but a hundred years later they're still hiding.'

'What are they so scared of?' I ask.

'The pox. Years ago your Lord Macawber led a team outside the walls to see if they could start saving the land and some of them got sick. The illness spread when they went back inside and hundreds died.' Connor shakes his head. 'It was a bad time. Karush blamed Macawber and when he used necromancy it was the perfect excuse to get rid of him.

Macawber was banished and Karush took over. He started throwing out anyone who was sick. People were so scared of the pox they let him and pretty soon he started casting out anyone who opposed him too.'

'Has the pox ever come back?'

'No. I think it was a one-off outbreak because the City had been closed for so long. Certainly the air outside offers us no problems. The outcasts suffer nothing worse than the odd chill, fever, infections . . .'

'It's not an easy life outside the walls though, is it?' Molly says, her hand trailing in the cool water. 'You can see why they'd rather hide inside their walls.'

'No, it's not easy but they can't hide in there for ever, can they? Eventually their supplies will run out, the magic will fade, and then what?' Connor's broad shoulders shift and move as he heaves the oars back and forth. 'They'd be better off working to restore the land and clean the water while they can.'

'If we don't get the locket to Ellari soon there will be no one left to do anything. The monsters will smash down the walls and kill everyone.'

'So you think this Ellari can stop them? With that magic locket of yours?'

'That's what my master said. She can drain the magic keeping them alive.' My eyes flick to my friends and I swallow. 'I wish there was another way but there isn't.'

Sherman catches my gaze and I see a grim understanding dawning there. My throat is so tight I can hardly breathe. He knows now what will happen when Ellari uses the locket but he nods his head slowly, accepting his fate, and I have to look away before I start sobbing.

'Well let's hurry up then!' Connor says. 'The sooner she gets it, the sooner we can get rid of all these undead abominations.'

'Then you'd better row faster, Pa,' Molly says.

Connor groans and pulls at the oars. 'I'm an old man you know, I'm not used to all this hard work.'

'Perhaps you should have spent less time drinking and gambling!' Molly replies.

'Now you sound like your ma!'

Molly pokes out her tongue. Connor laughs and so she splashes him with water.

They're still laughing at his dripping face when the not-actually-dead War Creature swings down from the ceiling and tries to snatch me from the boat.

19

I don't even move.

The creature that killed Patches swoops towards me on a long line of web, its great tubular head with a red, round maw gaping open and dripping with drool, its hairy black legs extended and reaching for me.

And I sit there like a statue with my mouth hanging open in a trapped scream, waiting for my doom to strike.

But something heavy knocks me backwards out of the creature's path and I feel my fate whistle past my head.

My brief moment of relief is shattered by Tingle's wail of sorrow.

'SHERMAN!'

Sherman, my friend, my saviour, is gone.

Snatched away in my place.

'Brat?' Molly helps me up. 'Are you all right?'

'Yes, but it took Sherman!'

Connor swears.

'There he is!' Molly stands and points up among the stalactites. When I peer closely I can see the monster wrapping long yellow thread around a wriggling shape hanging high above us, turning it into some sort of cocoon.

'Is that Sherman?'

'I think so. That thing is part spider. That's what they do to their prey, isn't it?' Molly says.

'LOOK OUT!' Connor yells as the monster finishes its task and swings down again. He flings himself at his daughter and the two of them tumble out of the boat and into the water, causing the arachnoid creature to miss its target once again.

I check for Tingle but she's not there and my heart lurches.

'Tingle!' I shout.

'Tingle go get Sherman!' she shouts back and I spy her climbing up the walls, her sharp claws embedded in the craggy rock.

'Brat!' Connor calls from where he's clinging to the edge of the boat. 'Get in the river quick.'

I shake my head. The thought of jumping into that cold black water makes me tremble.

'You're a sitting target!'

'I can't,' I hiss through clenched teeth. My fear fills up every part of me. It's too strong to overcome despite the risk of staying put.

Instead I lie flat in the bottom of the boat, holding tightly to an oar, my eyes trailing Tingle's progress up the sides and praying that Sherman can last inside that strange cocoon.

Tingle's nimble feet and agile monkey tail serve her well and she swings from stalactite to stalactite, unseen by the creature who is keeping its many eyes fixed on the prey in the river.

'IT'S COMING!' I shout as the arachnoid launches itself down once more.

Molly and Connor disappear beneath the water, but I am alone in the boat watching that vile monster fly towards me. I lash out with the oar, get lucky, and knock its fat round body away. It swings into the wall, hisses loudly, and then attacks once more.

This time the monster smashes the oar from my hands with one hairy leg and I am left helpless as it reaches for me.

I kick out in desperation, catching it in one of its eyes, and it shrieks with pain as hot liquid spills from the orb onto my foot.

It scrambles back up its long sticky web-line to recover and I pant and try not to vomit in the boat.

'Brat, you have to get in the water! Please!' Molly calls but I can't. However sensible it is, I can't do it.

The creature launches itself again, descending towards me, death shining in its remaining eyes.

I take one last look at Tingle, who's reached the ceiling now. As I watch she reaches for the monster's web-line and slices through it with one sharp claw.

The creature plummets into the river with an almighty splash, snatching at Molly as it goes. Connor rushes to her rescue.

Then, before I can stop her, Tingle slashes at the line holding Sherman and his cocoon falls like a stone and plunges into the depths, my shrill screams following him down.

He's going to drown. Just like my parents drowned and I can't bear it.

Sherman. My Sherman. My first friend.

He might be grumpy, slow, and permanently pessimistic but he is also brave and steady and true. Whatever might happen when we get to the City, I can't sit idly by and watch him drown. I will not let the water take anyone else from me.

I take a deep breath, close my eyes, and jump into the river after him.

The freezing darkness closes over my head and I have to fight the rising fear that threatens to overwhelm me and stop myself struggling back to the surface.

I have to save him.

I kick wildly and push myself down through the depths, eyes searching for any sign of Sherman.

Finally a glimmer of bright yellow shimmers from below but, as the air in my lungs disappears, it's harder and harder to keep swimming.

With a final burst of effort I reach the cocoon, grab it with my fingertips, and then kick up with all my might before my lungs explode.

My chest inflates with fresh air and the dizzy headache disappears. I ignore the chaos of the flailing creature as Molly and Connor fight against it with the broken oars.

I drag myself back to the boat and crawl in, pulling my friend behind me. I wipe my hand over the sticky strands suffocating Sherman and make a hole big enough for his head to fit through.

His panicked eyes find mine and I sob a little with relief. I did it. I saved him.

His long tongue swipes my face, licking at my tears, and my heart throbs with love and a tiny burst of pride. Maybe I'm not completely useless after all?

I huddle in the boat, freezing and exhausted, fresh blood leaking from my bandages. I look up to find Tingle clinging to a stalactite, her tiny face afraid. I may have saved Sherman but it's not enough. Now I need to think of a way to save us all.

The monster can't drown, the water is too pure to hurt him, and we have no weapons. Eventually we will tire and the monster will cocoon us all among the stone spines in the ceiling and feed on us at will.

And no one will warn the City and Ellari won't be able to save them and all of Niyandi Mor will die.

Unless . . .

'Tingle!' I shout. 'Break the stalactites!'

'What stalac . . . tites?' she calls.

'The spikes, the sharp spikes hanging from the ceiling, can you break them off? There, right over the monster?'

'I do it, Brat-Brat!'

'MOLLY! CONNOR!' I yell. 'Get away from the creature, quickly!'

They hear me and by some miracle do as I say, throwing their broken oars at the monster and swimming away just as Tingle dislodges the first few stone spears.

They hit the creature, he swipes at them angrily but now larger spikes are falling and slicing, smashing into its limbs over and over so it can't escape.

Tingle kicks her back legs at the largest stalactite and finally it cracks and plunges downwards, its pointed end stabbing its way through the creature's head and driving it down to the bottom of the river.

Black blood bubbles up to the surface and then the river goes still.

Molly and Connor climb into the boat, bruised and bloody from their fight. Tingle swings her way back down and throws herself at Sherman and starts licking his face.

Sherman doesn't even pretend to mind.

Connor reaches for a broken oar and paddles us the last few hundred yards to the jetty where a ladder hangs from the wall. A ladder that leads up to the City and some small piece of safety.

20

Exhausted, soaked, battered, and close to collapse, somehow we manage to make our way up the ladder, through the hatch, and into the water control room that sits above.

'There won't be anyone here now,' Connor reassures us. 'It's the middle of the night.'

I slam the hatch down with a shiver, the memory of that monster still lingering, and follow Connor as he makes his way through a mass of pipes to a small alcove with a roughly made bed inside.

'Useful for the odd daytime nap this was.'

'No time for sleeping now though,' Molly says.

'Maybe not but we need to at least get dry and eat something before we go up. Go through there to the stores, my lovely, should be some dry clothes and food.' He eases himself back onto the bed with a wince.

'Come with me, Brat.' Molly grabs my arm and pulls me through the door with her.

Faint mage-light glimmers when we step inside the vast underground stores. The huge chamber is filled with shelf upon shelf of supplies and I feel a bit dizzy staring at all the things they have.

'Stars and moon!' Molly breathes, taking it all in.

'I know.'

'They have so much! And they're still throwing people out into the wastes!' Molly storms off searching for what we need.

I walk slowly behind trying to imagine why they feel the need to banish people when their shelves hold enough food and supplies to last a lifetime.

'Got some clothes!' Molly shouts. 'They're horrid but they are dry.'

'Good!' I yell back through chattering teeth.

I grab a few jars and packets from the

shelves and together we head back to the alcove.

Molly and I strip off under blankets and put on the hessian overalls and undershirts she found.

'It's like some horrible uniform,' Molly says, staring down at herself.

'It's what all the Domers wear so you'll fit right in,' Connor says. 'Only the rich council men who support Karush and vote on his cursed policies get to wear anything different.'

'Well, it's good to be dry at least. Your turn now, Pa, I got you a bigger size.'

'I'm fine, Molly love.'

'Don't be silly! You'll catch a chill in those wet things.'

I sit on the floor and fix my bandages while Molly argues with Connor.

When he finally takes his shirt off, I hear Molly gasp with horror.

'Pa! Why didn't you say you were hurt?'

'I'm fine Mols. It's just a scratch!'

It's more than a scratch. A long, weeping, red wound runs from chest to hip. The creature must have caught him with a taloned foot during their fight.

I go and forage for more bandages in the stores but there isn't much in the way of healing supplies. In the end we wash the injury with a flask of old wine I manage to find and bandage it tightly with a ripped-up uniform. I give Connor the rest of the flask to help him with the pain he's pretending not to feel.

Despite Molly's urging, Connor barely eats the small meal we prepare but he drains half the wine.

'How do you feel?' I ask him.

'Not so good,' he admits, his face growing flush and red with fever.

'It's wound rot, isn't it?' Molly demands of me.

'I think so. A bit like what I had. Maybe it's the War Creature's dead flesh that spreads it?'

'So, we need a healer then?'

I bite my lip. 'Or some of that medicine they use at least.'

Molly stands up. 'Right, then we'll go up now and get some on the way to find Ellari.'

'I can't go up there,' Connor says.

'We'll help you!'

He shakes his head. 'No, I can't make it, Mols. Trust me, I know.'

'But we can't go up there without you!' Her voice is high and scared.

'It's all right, Mols,' Connor says. 'I told you I had a contact in the City, didn't I? He's in the office opposite. Farrell's in charge of keeping records. Tell him I sent you. He'll help you get where you need to go.'

Molly bends down next to her pa. 'But I don't want to leave you!'

'I know, but you have to, my petal, this is important. Don't worry, I'll be fine, Tingle and Sherman will look after me.'

'Tingle want go with Brat-Brat!' she says, jumping on my shoulder.

'You can't,' Connor says. 'You two would stand out a mile! You'd be caught in five minutes and thrown out the gates.'

'Not fair,' Tingle grumbles.

I don't want to leave them either but I can't put the mission at risk. We have to get to Ellari before the monsters arrive.

'You get to stay down here with all the

food, Tingle!' I tell her.

'And you need to look after my pa,' Molly says. 'You will, won't you?'

'Tingle very good at looking after,' she says, puffing out her chest and then licking her lips. 'And eating.'

I squeeze her in my arms and breathe in the sweet smell of her fur, trying not to think about what will happen if I succeed. If we actually get to Ellari and she uses the locket to drain the magic . . .

'Bye-bye, Tingle, be good,' I whisper, a stray tear leaking from my eye and falling into her fur.

'Tingle always good!' she says, jumping over to the bed to get petted by Connor.

I bend down and stroke Sherman. His tongue unfurls and slurps around my face, licking the stray tears away.

'Brat Sherman's best friend,' he says softly.

'But . . .' I want to ask him, to know if I'm doing the right thing, if he's sure, but I can't speak. I can barely swallow.

'Is OK, Brat. Promise.'

I kiss his ugly beautiful face. 'Look after

Tingle,' I whisper and he nods and I stand up and walk away before Molly can see how unbearably sad I am.

21

Twenty minutes later, our hair hidden by the uniform hats Connor made us find, we head through the stores to the stairway at the end.

Halfway up the metal rungs nailed to the wall, we're both panting and out of breath, and Connor's insistence that he wouldn't make it now seems obvious. There is a pulley system for hauling up the boxes and stores but I'm pretty sure we wouldn't have the strength to haul Connor or even Sherman that far up.

By the time we make it to the top I'm about ready to collapse entirely, until we step outside and I get my first glimpse of the City.

Molly and I stand there, staring upwards with our mouths open as we take in the enormous glass roof that covers the entire City.

I can see the bright dawn sun but its warmth is muted and there's no breath of wind. Instead the air feels stale and dry.

The walls that support the giant dome rise up five times the height of the tallest man. Perfectly smooth and immensely thick, they encircle a vast space, far bigger than I'd imagined.

It's my first glimpse of what magic is truly capable of and I can see why they feel safe in here. Why my master had to create what he did. Only magical creatures would stand any chance of getting through these walls.

Molly grabs my arm and pulls me back against the building.

'People!' she hisses, and I see a group of uniformed workers make their way past us and head towards the fields that fill the city almost to the horizon. Trees and bushes and plants fill my gaze like an explosion of green.

'Look at all that fresh food!' I hiss at Molly. 'There's acres of it!'

'Yes, and they hoard it all like proper misers. Every plum and apple counted and filed away.'

I watch as more and more people start

arriving for work. The fields are soon full of workers; weeding, planting, watering, and harvesting.

Strangely, despite the bustle of work there's very little chatter, no laughter, no songs, nothing. The people seem muted, nervous, and barely look up from their tasks.

The only people I see not actually working in the fields are patrolling them instead with clipboards in their hands and a blue band across their uniforms. The overseers. Connor said they were the ones to watch out for. They see everything, note it, and report it back to Karush.

A young woman with red-rimmed eyes and straggly hair rushes past me and Molly and into the fields.

A tall, male overseer approaches.

'You're nine minutes late for your shift. Name?' he demands.

'Please, I'm sorry. My son is sick . . . please don't report me.'

'Name?' the overseer demands again, completely unmoved by her plea.

'I'm begging you, please, I'll do anything!'

She grasps at the man's arm but he brushes her away like an annoying fly.

'Name, now, or I'll penalize you double!'

The young woman shows him a band on her wrist and he jots something down on his paper.

'The health inspector will be over later to check your son poses no risk to the City,' he tells her and she starts work with tears dripping down her face.

'Stop gawping will you?' Molly snaps. 'We've got to go.'

'Right, sorry.'

I follow Molly as she crosses over the street to the building opposite. It's one of many; tall and grey and soulless. Homes for the many workers I assume.

'More ruddy stairs!' Molly says, looking at a board outside with the floor numbers on. 'Record keeping is on the fourth floor, come on.'

We make our way up the steps, not talking. Each of us is caught up in our own worries. On the fourth-floor landing I stop.

'What is it?' Molly asks. 'We're nearly

there!'

'I know. I just . . . thank you, Molly.'

'What?'

'For helping me.' I need to tell her, just in case I don't get a chance later. 'I've never known anyone like you, brave and kind and strong, and I'd never have got here, inside the City, without you so . . . thank you.'

Molly's cheeks turn red. 'That's what friends are for, Brat.'

'You mean . . .' I swallow. 'Are we friends then? Really?'

'Brat! Of course we are, you big barnacle head!'

'I've never had a proper friend before. A human one, I mean.'

'Well, I'm honoured to be the first. Really. If I had to go on this terrible adventure with anyone, I'm glad it was you.'

I feel my own face growing hot at her words and I can't stop smiling.

'Now how about we get on with saving the world and leave the soppy stuff for later?'

I nod, wishing that somehow, someway, there might actually be a later, for all of us.

Molly pushes the door open and we step inside the dim and draughty room. Piles of papers line the walls, in boxes and files, great towers that look like they might fall at any moment

A sharp cough catches our attention and we follow the sound to a large desk, almost lost in the middle of the chaos.

'How may I be of service?' says the man sitting behind it, barely visible behind the stacks of documents. He's almost as grey as the room.

'We're looking for Farrell?' Molly says, her eyes searching for someone else, someone who looks more suited to rebellion.

'I'm Farrell,' the man says, smoothing back his thinning grey hair.

'You're the smuggler?'

'SSHHHHH!' he barks, leaping up to slam the door shut behind us.

'Umm, Connor sent us . . .'

'This is most irregular! Who are you?' He peers at us both.

'I'm his daughter Molly, this is Brat.'

'What are you doing in the City?' he hisses.

'If you're found . . .'

'We know. But we have no choice. My father said you'd help us.'

'Help you what?'

'We need to find Ellari, and we need a healer, and we need to find them both now.'

Farrell frowns.

'Please?' I ask. 'It's important.'

'Fine, I'll tell you where to go but that's it. And if you're caught you never heard of me, got it?'

22

We follow Farrell's rough map through the streets, keeping our eyes down and trying to act as if we belong. We find the ramshackle house marked with an X but neither of us are ready to go in.

'What if it's a trap?' Molly asks. 'I didn't trust that Farrell.'

'He was just scared. Helping us is a big risk.'

'Do you really think Ellari is inside then?'

'He said she ran a clinic here every morning. If it's true we can get the medicine AND give her the locket.'

'Then let's do it. I'm worried about Pa.' She pushes the door and pulls me inside with her.

'Hello?' Molly calls.

'Yes?' A young fair-haired woman sits behind a table in a large echoey room.

'We've come to find a healer?'

'That's me, how can I help?' She smiles briefly.

'You're Ellari Macawber!' I say when I move closer. She looks exactly the same as she did. Only the mischievous spark in her eyes is gone, replaced by something darker.

Ellari frowns and stands up. 'How do you know that name?'

'I've seen your picture . . .' I take the locket out from under my tunic and open it.

'That was my mother's locket!' Ellari says, stepping closer. 'Where did you get it?'

'From your father.'

She swallows hard. 'My father? When . . . when did he give it to you?'

'A few days ago . . . just before he died.'

She stumbles back and sits on her desk, face pale.

'Who are you?' she asks with a hoarse voice.

'I'm Brat. I lived with your pa for the last few years, helping with his experiments.'

'You mean you're from outside the City? How did you get in?'

'It doesn't matter. We've come a long way to find you.'

'Why? To tell me my father is dead?'

'Because you're our only hope . . .' I don't know where to start but Molly blurts out the whole story in a long rush of words, hardly stopping for breath.

'. . . so you have to help us. I need medicine for my pa, he has the wound rot from fighting that spider monster in the river and then you need to use that locket to drain the magic from the War Creature army and save the world.'

When Molly finally stops talking, the room falls silent and still.

'Monsters?' Ellari says eventually.

'Yes.'

'That's what my father has been doing for the last seven years? Using necromancy to make a monster army so he could come and rescue me?' Disbelief drips from her words.

'Yes.'

'But that's insane!'

I wince. 'He was a bit unhinged by what

happened.'

'But . . . really? Seriously? Monsters?'

'I know it's hard to believe. I can hardly believe it and I've seen them with my own eyes.' Molly says.

'He was desperate to get you back,' I say.

Ellari shakes her head. 'No. He wasn't.'

'He was! He talked about you all the time. He dedicated his life to making those monsters. For the last year he never left his laboratory.' Some of my bitterness leaks through my words.

'If he really loved me he could have come back any time,' she says.

I open my mouth to disagree but no words come out.

'Look at you, Brat, you got into the City and found me without any cursed monster army and you're just a child! My father was a mage! It would have been easy for him.'

'But . . . why then . . . ?' Molly asks.

'Revenge,' she says with a big sigh. 'That's why he did it. He and Lord Karush were bitter rivals for years. When Karush finally won it must have driven him mad. The idea of marching back to the City with a magical army, smashing down the walls, and destroying his enemy was what truly drove him. Not me. I was just an excuse.'

'No . . . he loved you. He did.'

'He left me behind voluntarily, Brat. He didn't have to.' She sounds so sad, so lonely.

'He wanted you to be safe . . .' I say but I don't know why I'm defending him. Ellari's version sounds horribly true.

'Safe? Yes I suppose I was safe . . . until now of course when the monsters my father made have come to kill me.' She laughs but it's a hollow sound.

'I'm sorry,' I mutter.

'It's not your fault, is it?' She gets up and moves over to her worktable. 'I'll make a poultice for your father, Molly, it should draw out the poison and help the wound heal faster. There's a tea I can give you to help with any fever.'

'Thank you,' Molly says quietly.

'No problem,' she says, pouring seeds into a mortar and grinding the contents with a pestle, concentration across her brow. 'I add a little of my magic to the medicine and that helps its effectiveness. Your . . . friends, the ones you mentioned . . . . are they looking after him?'

'Yes, Tingle and Sherman. Your father made them first, as an experiment just to see if he could. They worked but weren't any use to him so I took them. They're my best friends in the world.'

'Charming,' Molly mutters under her breath.

'Oh, and Molly now too of course. I'd never have got here without her, she's amazing.'

Molly blushes slightly and gives me a small grin.

'But the other experiments . . . they're not the same?'

'No. Your father made them from real monsters hunted and killed across the sea; ogres and arachnids and gatoricus and everything. He thought he could control them but the last one drained his magic and then it killed him and now they're all loose and coming here.'

Ellari takes a deep breath. 'And the mad fool said I could stop them?'

'You have magic. You can activate the locket to drain them. It's the only way to stop them.'

'But I don't know how to do that!'

She spoons the contents of the mortar onto a poultice made of leaves and runs her hand over it, making it glow.

'The only thing I'm really good at is healing. I sneak out of the house every few days to run this clinic and offer people some small aid. Karush prefers to keep me caged at home, my magic used only at his command but I can't just let people suffer, can I?' She starts measuring more ingredients. 'And I know how to help the crops grow and preserve the food in the stores and charge the lights but that's it. There was no one to teach me how to use proper magic, no one else even can.'

'Aren't there any books and scrolls on magic here?'

'No,' her lip curls. 'Karush burnt them years ago so I wouldn't take any risks.'

'More like he didn't want you learning enough magic to be able to challenge him like your father did,' I suggest.

'Well, my father was wrong, wasn't he? He tried to make people go outside and the pox could have killed us all.'

'But it didn't. Most people survived.'

'Only because Karush threw the sick outside and stopped it spreading.'

'But if the air outside is so dangerous, how come we're not sick?' Molly asks. 'There are hundreds of people living outside the walls and none of us have the pox!'

Ellari frowns. 'Is that true? There are so many of you?'

'Yes. We've made settlements on the coast, we live well and free. My ma even grows her own vegetables in earth she has made fertile.'

'That's impossible! The land is scorched, poisoned. Nothing will grow.'

'With the right fertilizer and enough work it can! Ellari, this city isn't a haven, it's more like a prison,' Molly says. 'I saw the workers, they look miserable. You all look miserable. You're all trapped and living in fear.'

'And Karush is now throwing people out when they're not even sick! When they pose no threat.' I add.

'He says only the hardworking and loyal deserve the safety of the walls,' Ellari says in a small voice.

'Loyal to him, you mean. Anyone who disagrees with him is thrown outside and you all let him do it.'

Ellari looks anguished. 'I . . . I know. You're right but it's not that easy. You don't know what he's like. No one challenges him.'

'They're all too scared!' Molly says. 'You could challenge him though! You have magic—he's not going to cast you out, is he? Without you he's nothing. The whole city will collapse.'

I watch Ellari struggle with her conscience. She's more like me than I ever thought. An orphan. Alone, desperate to be loved, and forced to help someone do something she knows is wrong but too scared to stop.

'No one would listen to me,' she says. 'I'm not important, not really. I'm just a silly girl with a gift. I need someone to tell me what to do, to make the decisions.'

'You don't really believe that,' I say. 'You wouldn't be here running this clinic behind his back if that's what you thought. You're stronger than you think, Ellari.'

I take the locket from my pocket and hold it out to her. 'It's yours. The only thing standing between us and the monsters. You have to use it when they come. Please.'

Ellari hesitates, her fingers reach out to take it . . .

'Get away from my daughter you outcast scum!' The doors fly open with a bang and Lord Karush drags Ellari away from me and the locket.

23

So close! Damn Lord Karush and his cursed spies.

'What do you think you're doing?' he snaps at Ellari.

'I . . .'

'Do you want the pox? Is that what you want?'

'No but . . .'

'Then you stay away from these disgusting disease-carrying outcasts, do you hear me?'

He waves his hand and three blank-faced overseers march in and bind our hands behind our backs. I keep the locket tightly clenched in my fist.

'Did you think you wouldn't be noticed?' he demands of us. 'I know everything that happens in my city. Everything!'

'We came to help,' Molly says but Karush isn't listening.

'I am sick of your kind! How dare you put my daughter at risk! How dare you sneak into MY city with your filthy, disgusting germs!'

I don't know what I expected of Lord Karush.

The way everyone spoke about him I imagined someone tall and broad and threatening but in real life he's short and paunchy and going bald and I think Molly could probably knock him out if she tried. But despite his looks, there is something dark and sinister hiding in his eyes. The force of his personality is strong enough to overwhelm all others.

'Father, please . . .' Ellari says.

'I don't need to hear ANOTHER WORD from you!' he spits. 'Obviously you can't be trusted! It's bad enough you go behind my back with this . . . "clinic" . . . of yours but to put us all in danger by associating with outcasts!'

Ellari gulps but doesn't back down. 'Father,

they're not the real danger here!'

'Yes, they are! They're walking germ factories,' he shouts, spittle flying from his mouth. 'And they're going straight back out the gates in this morning's outcasting! Just as soon as they've divulged how they got in here!'

Karush glares at us both. 'So? How did you get in to my city? Who helped you? You'd best tell me now or you'll regret it I assure you!'

Molly and I stay quiet. We can't give up Connor and Tingle and Sherman or Farrell.

Karush reaches out a hand and grabs Molly's face, squeezing it between his fingers. 'Speak out, little girl! How did you get in? I won't have everything I've worked for over the years put at risk by you disgusting sewer rats!'

'Leave her alone!' I shout. 'Don't hurt her!'

Karush shoves Molly away from him. 'Then tell me how you got in! I know there's been illegal smuggling going on for years and I will not have it! I'll seal up every hole and every gap until this city is safe from your kind once and for all!'

His eyes are wild. Fear and panic pulse inside each pupil. He really believes it. I thought he was using the threat of the pox as a way of keeping his power but he's actually afraid. That's what's driving his cruel policies.

He spots the package of medicine Ellari left on the table. 'You came here for healing, didn't you? Someone is sick.'

He lifts the parcel in his hands.

'Are they hiding somewhere in my city? Are they festering away in the dark, spreading their sickness?'

Molly bites her lip. Connor needs that medicine but he won't get it now without being captured by Karush.

'Tell me where they are!' Karush shouts. 'Tell me where they are right now and . . . I'll let you take the medicine with you when I throw you out.'

Molly flicks me a glance but I don't know what to do either.

'If you don't tell me, they'll die, slowly and alone.' He prowls around the room, the package in his hands.

'All right!' Molly says. 'But I'll only tell

Ellari and she has to go and get my father and give him that medicine.'

'I'm not putting my daughter at risk for one of your kind!'

'But I don't mind going, Father,' Ellari says.

'NO ONE ASKED YOU!' he bellows at her and she cowers from his rage like a kicked puppy.

'He's not sick though, he's hurt, injured,' Molly says. 'There's no risk to Ellari, I swear.'

Karush sniffs. 'Very well then. As long as I find out the route you rats are using I don't really care. I will stamp out this perfidious smuggling once and for all.'

'There are worse things to worry about than smuggling, you fool! We didn't come here just for medicine, we came to warn you!'

Karush ignores me, too focused on his own obsessions. Just like my master. Both of them ignoring what is good and right, both of them destroying lives in order to achieve their own selfish ambitions. And neither of them listening to reason.

He addresses his minions. 'Take them

down to the gates. Put them with the other outcasts and follow Ellari when she goes to fetch the rest of the scum who tried to sneak into my city!'

24

The overseers march us across the City and push Molly and me inside a large tent set up near the walls. We stumble into a miserable throng of fifteen other people who barely register our presence.

'What's going on?' I whisper to Molly. 'Who are they?'

'They must be the other people being cast out today.'

'Oh.' I can almost smell the despair.

'Pa said they check their records every third month. Those who've missed work, been late, failed to meet their quota, are all at risk. Also anyone who's been on report to the overseers for disloyalty, drunkenness, or disruptive behaviour can be added to the list too.'

'So, these people just found out they were on the list today?'

'Some of them may have guessed. But they found out for sure this morning when an overseer went to their houses and brought them to the tent.'

'And they don't get to say goodbye to their families?' I ask. 'Their friends? They don't get to take anything with them?'

Molly shakes her head. I know she's thinking about her parents. This happened to Connor and Cassy.

It's so barbaric. At first it seems like they have everything here: food, security, supplies, but really they're all living under a constant cloud of fear.

That fear has warped their city. Kept them locked inside, hiding from the world instead of helping to shape it, made them turn their backs on others to save themselves.

I knew what that felt like. I'd let fear keep me locked in the castle and I only acted when I was forced to. I put people at risk but I won't let fear control me any more.

I've seen what happens when people work

together. The outcasts were thrown out, left for dead, but instead of giving up they had worked together and found a way to live well and try and improve all of Niyandi Mor. And Molly and Connor had risked their lives to help me save the very people who had hurt them so much.

The tent flap opens again and Tingle comes flying through. She throws herself at my head and curls her tail so tight around my neck I can barely breathe.

'Brat-Brat! Tingle miss you! Bad men come, Brat-Brat, and Tingle scratched them up but they was very mean and put Tingle in a bag! Tingle not like bag!'

I can't stop the burst of joy that rushes through me at being with her again. Sherman butts at my legs so I sit down and let him climb onto my lap. I hold them tightly, enjoying every second, determined to make whatever time we have left together as full of love as possible.

Tingle chatters in my ear but I barely listen, my head is full of memories. Of when I first found them and when they came to my room and the nights of snuggling in my bed and ignoring Sherman's farts and Tingle's raspy tongue on my face each morning.

Molly gives a squeak of joy when Connor joins us in the tent. He looks better than before. I think Ellari must have got to him and managed to heal him a little and I'm glad. Seeing Molly together with her pa makes me happy. I can almost imagine how it must feel to have a family who love you and it makes me feel stronger. It gives me hope.

'So,' Connor says. 'What happens now? Are the miserable cowards going to throw us out?'

'Well, we won't let them. We'll just tell them why we're here and they'll have to listen to us,' Molly says.

'It's not that easy,' Connor says. 'I've been here before, remember? Karush makes his speech, reads out the names and the crimes, and then they push the outcasts through the gate as fast as they can. All the Domers left behind feel grateful and lucky for a while and then the cycle starts again.'

'Well, we have to do something! We can't

fail now.'

'And we can't let them throw anyone out,' Connor says. 'Not with those monsters on their way!'

'We distract them,' I say. 'And we get the locket to Ellari. That's the only thing that matters.'

'Do you really think you can trust her, Brat?' Connor asks. 'She basically just let her father arrest you and now she's going to let him throw you outside. She doesn't seem brave enough to do anything!'

'She'll use the locket if we can get it to her. She'll get rid of the monsters. I know she will.'

'Maybe we should have a back-up plan?' Connor suggests.

'There's no time,' I say, a strange sense of calm descending over me.

'Why not?'

I point at the grass at my feet, the faint tremble that ripples through it at every. Single. Foot. Step.

'Because the monsters are nearly here.'

25

A loud bell rings out almost on cue. It clangs twelve times.

Everyone in the tent tenses up.

'It's noon, the ceremony starts now,' Connor whispers.

As the final note dies away, Karush's voice rings out. 'My people! I have promised always to keep you safe. It isn't easy. I have to be constantly vigilant. Constantly on guard. But the events of this morning have reminded me exactly how important that is! I have to tell you that a few hours ago a band of filthy outcasts were discovered INSIDE our beautiful city!'

We hear gasps and cries from the crowds outside and then three overseers march in and grab me, Molly, Connor, Tingle, and Sherman and drag us from the tent.

Hundreds of people stare at us as we emerge. Some of them boo. And hiss. Karush is standing on a small stage near the wall with Ellari and a few others seated on chairs behind him.

'They were found amongst our stores, trying to steal from us . . .' Karush continues.

'That's a lie! We came to—' Whatever Connor was trying to say is lost when an overseer hits him in the face. Molly kicks the bully in the shin and gets a backhanded slap for her trouble.

'As you can see, they are a gang of violent thugs and mutant beasts and must be dealt with swiftly. Open the gates!' Karush calls.

'Please listen! We came to warn you!' I shout but my voice is drowned out by the cheering of the crowds. I can't believe we're going to fail in our mission when we came so close! Why won't they listen?

'STOP!' Ellari's strong voice cuts through the noise and the crowd falls silent, the gate stops opening. 'It's not true. They didn't come to steal from us—they came to warn us of danger.'

'Ellari! How dare you!' Karush demands. 'Sit back down right now, young lady!'

I hold my breath. Can Ellari really stand up to him for once? I will her to be strong. To find a way.

'No, Father. Not this time. The people need to know that a dangerous army of monsters is coming for us.'

Karush gapes at Ellari.

'What nonsense is this? Are you deranged, girl?'

'It's true!' I shout, finding my voice at last and letting it ring out across the crowds. I will not be afraid any more. I will not be silenced. Not ever again. 'Lord Macawber made them from the parts of dead monsters and used necromancy to bring them back to life. He designed them so they could destroy your walls and kill you all in revenge for you banishing him all those years ago!'

'Macawber?' Karush splutters. 'That addle-brained fool? I don't believe it.'

'Then maybe you should listen for once, Lord Karush,' I say. 'They're already here.'

A hush settles over the City and there,

unmistakably, comes the deep and heavy thud of a marching army and a faint, menacing roaring.

Panicked mutterings break out among the people.

'We have nothing to fear!' Karush promises the crowds. 'Our walls can withstand any army! We are more at risk from these filthy reprobates so we will rid ourselves of them now!'

'If you throw them out, I go with them,' Ellari says and she walks right past him to stand with us.

'How dare you defy me!' Karush snarls. 'After everything I've done for you all these years!'

'What you did for me? What about what I do for you? You only kept me beside you because of my magic. Because you knew without me this city would crumble! I won't stand by and let you throw these children into danger after they came all this way to give warning.'

Karush clenches his jaw so tight I think it might break. He knows Ellari speaks the truth. He needs her. The whole city needs her and she's finally taking control of her power.

'In fact,' Ellari says, almost giddy with her own rebellion, 'I won't let you throw anyone out again! It's cruel and it's wrong to live this way.'

'Don't tell me what I can or cannot do! I've kept the people of this city safe for years. It was I who saved us when YOUR FATHER nearly destroyed us!' He turns to address the crowds. 'I am telling you all, the walls keep us safe! Getting rid of the sick and the lazy keeps us safe!'

A loud hammering sounds as the army reaches the walls and begins their assault. The Domers cower at the noise and I wonder what they'd do if they could actually see the horrific monsters waiting outside.

'There is nothing to fear!' Karush insists. 'You can trust me—my word is as strong as this very dome!'

And just then there's a sharp cracking sound and a long fissure appears in the dome above the gates. It travels up and up, racing across the entire roof, spreading further with every mighty pound on the walls.

Karush falls silent, his eyes following the

trail, his mouth gaping open. The deception of his words has never been more obvious.

They cannot trust Karush.

And they are very definitely not safe.

Panic shoots through the crowd and they start screaming and running but there is nowhere for them to go. Danger lies above and beyond.

Karush offers no solutions. His face is locked in a hideous grimace of disbelief as his beloved city starts to fail right before his eyes.

I look over at Ellari. She's calm, on the outside at least.

'Untie the prisoners,' she demands of a passing overseer and her tone is so confident he obeys.

We rub at our wrists and watch as chaos takes over.

'Give her the locket, Brat!' Molly says. 'Stop the monsters.'

'But that dome could fall at any minute!' I say. 'We have to get everyone somewhere safe before we worry about the monsters.'

'But there's nowhere to go!' Molly shouts over the rising noise.

'Tingle not like it here!' Tingle says, scratching her way up my leg. 'Tingle want to go!'

'I know but the monsters are outside!'

'We go to the food,' she says firmly. 'Tingle hungry.' The answer rushes into my head and I give Tingle a big kiss on her greedy wet nose.

'You have to order an evacuation, Ellari! Quickly.'

She nods. 'Agreed, but where to?'

'Down. Through the stores to the underground river. They can get all the way to Arberra that way!'

'That's perfect, Brat!' She nods her head. 'We'll get everyone to safety and then I'll use the locket on the monsters.'

'How are you going to get this lot to listen?' Molly asks, pointing at the panicked masses. 'They're not exactly calm.'

'Use the overseers,' Connor suggests. 'The Domers are used to listening to them.'

'Perfect!' Ellari says. 'I'll give them their orders and they can corral everyone down to the stores.'

'And then I'll show them the way down to the river,' Connor says.

'I'll go and get the other outcasts from the tent,' Molly says. 'They deserve a chance to escape too.'

While the others rush away to organize the evacuation I retreat and sit quietly in a doorway out of sight, holding onto my friends. The time is coming. I know it has to, I know there's no other choice and it has to be done, but now we're finally here I just wish we could run away again.

I think Sherman can feel me trembling; he raises his head from my lap to look at me. 'Don't be afraid, Brat, this is not the end'.

I smile a sad smile. He would know. He's done this before. I squeeze him a little tighter in my arms. At least this time we're together.

26

With the promise of escape, the citizens swiftly follow orders and soon the City is all but empty. The only noise now is the steady, remorseless thump of the monsters pounding at the walls.

Mortar is falling, chips and chunks and dust scatter the ground. Whatever magic is in the walls cannot stand up to this pitched assault for long.

When I look up I can see a forest of tiny cracks have spread across the dome. It shimmers and shakes with every heavy bash and I don't think it will be long until the glass begins to fall.

'Brat!' Molly runs over. 'There you are.'

'How's the evacuation going?' I ask, trying

hard to keep my voice normal.

'Good. We're sending them through the river on barrels and they're clearing out the storerooms as they go. We'll need the extra food and supplies to cope with all the new people.'

'It will be a shock for the Domers, won't it? Living outside.'

'Well, they don't have much choice, do they? Their city will soon be destroyed. It looks like the walls will fall any minute.'

I nod. 'Soon.'

Ellari joins us. 'Sorry! I had to help Karush get down to the stores. He's not coping very well at all with the destruction of his precious city. I'm ready now.'

I get up and hand the locket over to Ellari, trying to keep my hand from trembling.

She holds it in her palm.

'So, I should activate it now then? And what? The magic will be drained from the monsters all in one go?'

'I don't really know. Macawber didn't have time to say much.' I can't look at them. I bend down and stroke Tingle.

'All right, well, I'll just have to try I guess.'

'Wait,' Molly says. 'All the monsters? But . . . that means . . . Brat?'

I look up. 'Yes?'

She's staring at Tingle and Sherman. 'Does that mean what I think it means?'

Damn Molly! Why did she have to notice? It's easier if she doesn't know.

I let out a sigh. 'Yes. It will drain the magic from all the creatures who are alive because of necromancy.'

'But how can you let . . . ?' She looks down at my friends, wondering how I can sacrifice them both, how I can bear to lose them.

I swallow hard. 'All of them, Molly. Including me.'

'What? No! Brat, what do you mean?' Molly asks.

'Don't you see, Molly?' The truth burns my throat as it comes out at last. 'When I washed up on that shore I was dead! Drowned like my ma and pa but Lord Macawber used his cursed necromancy to bring me back to life!'

I turn my face away from her. 'I'm one of them,' I confess. 'It's why I thought I wouldn't be welcome in your village. I thought you'd all see it somehow, the thing inside that makes me a monster . . .'

I wait for the gasps of shock and horror but none come.

'Necromancy doesn't make you a monster!' Molly says without any pause at all. 'Doing evil makes you a monster and you have done nothing but good, Brat. You are better than all of us—kinder, braver, stronger.' Her hand slips into mine and squeezes.

I glance at her face, expecting at least a flicker of hatred or repulsion but she only smiles at me like she has always smiled at me and in her eyes there is . . . acceptance? Pride?

I should be happy, but there's more she doesn't know.

'No, Molly, you don't understand. I was the one who started this! It's all my fault. Macawber failed to bring his wife back to life but his magic worked with me! That's what made him begin his experiments, he told me so himself.' I shake my head. 'The world would have been better off if I had died that day with my ma and pa, then none of this would have happened!'

'Brat, that's not true,' Molly says but it is. I know it is.

'I've tried to use my stolen life for good, to do my best to make up for what I started but I messed it all up. I helped Lord Macawber because I wanted him to love me but I should have left years ago and told someone what he planned. I should have stopped him before all this could have happened. But I didn't. So I tried my best to warn everyone, and bring the locket here so you could all be saved.'

'Everyone but you?'

'It's the only way to keep you all safe,' I tell her, though the lump in my throat is hard to talk past. 'I want you all to be safe, you and Connor and Cassy and everyone. You welcomed me when I thought no one would, you helped me see what bravery was. I want you to have a future safe from monsters.'

'No, Brat! This isn't right. It's not your fault. Macawber made that army, not you! He is responsible, not you! We can think of something else, another plan! We can run too!'

'They'll find us, Molly. You know they will. This is the only answer, the only way to save everyone.'

'Sometimes ridding the world of evil takes sacrifice, Molly, like when the mages defeated the Magestreki,' Sherman says, as wise as ever.

'But that's not fair!' she shouts, fury and pain in her eyes. 'Why should you all have to die so we can live?'

I don't know. I don't know why and it isn't fair and I'm so scared but I don't say any of those things.

'It's fine,' I tell Molly, trying to make it easier for her somehow.

'It is not fine!' Molly stamps her foot, angry tears falling down her face.

'Don't cry, Molly!' Tingle says and I'm not sure she really understands what's happening but she puts her trust in me just like always. 'Tingle love you. Tingle be very brave for you.'

Her words only make Molly cry harder. 'This isn't your burden! You don't deserve to

die, none of you do. I don't want you to die!
You're my best friends, my only friends.'

'Don't be silly, Molly! You have a ma and
a pa, you have Kendrick and everyone in
your village. I'm doing this so you can all be
together. So you can be happy.'

Molly screws up her face. 'I won't be happy
without you! And I won't stay here and watch!'

She runs away and I let her. It's easier
this way. I don't want to admit how much I
want to stay. How much I want the chance
of a normal life. To stay with Molly and the
others and work outside and tell stories and
hug my friends and laugh at silly jokes . . . but
it's not my fate.

I suppose it never was.

The wall begins to crumble. There's only
minutes left.

I stroke Tingle for the last time, my fingers
enjoying the feel of her soft fur.

'Tingle not like it here, Brat-Brat,' she says.

'It's all right,' I whisper in her ear. 'We're
not staying long. You, me, and Sherman we're
going somewhere else very soon and we're
not coming back.'

'Tingle stay with Brat-Brat?' she says, licking the end of my nose with her raspy pink tongue and catching my tears.

'Yes. We'll be together, that's the important thing.'

'Brat, are you sure about this?' Ellari asks, looking horrified.

'As soon as I figured out how the locket worked I knew this was what had to happen.' I look down at Sherman. His steady gaze gives me the strength to carry on. We're doing the right thing.

'You came here willing to sacrifice yourselves to save all of us?' Ellari's voice echoes into the silence of the empty city.

I nod.

'That's the bravest thing I've ever heard.'

I shrug. 'You were pretty brave today. Standing up to Karush. Standing up for us. I knew you had it in you.'

Ellari smiles. 'How did you know? I certainly didn't!'

'Because if I could do it, if I could travel across Niyandi Mor to try and save people even though I'm useless and afraid, then I knew you would stand up to Karush to save us. Sometimes, the things we can't do for our own sakes we can do for others.'

She looks down at the locket in her hand. 'I don't want to do this, Brat. I don't want to be the one who . . .'

'I know. I'm sorry it has to be you but you have to be brave again, you have to help me save everyone.'

The walls by the gate collapse in a shower of dust, and wild bellows and roaring fill the air.

'Stars and moon . . .' Ellari gasps as she gets her first glimpse of the army.

'Greetings, humans! Welcome to your death!' Wrath's voice echoes in my ears like the chimes of doom.

They flood into the City, beasts of all shapes and sizes, a sea of teeth and claws and death. The lack of people soon becomes clear and they snarl and spit their frustration.

'You can hide, mortals! But we will find you! And you will die!' Wrath promises.

'Meanie stinkers!' Tingle screeches.

I press her head against my neck. 'Sssh. It's

all right. It will be over soon.'

Ellari is looking sick as the army rampages through the City, her mouth is agape. 'My father did this? He did this in my name?'

'You can stop them! Do it now, Ellari! Now!'

Ellari gulps and holds the locket up. She closes her eyes, tries to activate the magic.

But nothing happens. Just as before when Wrath got loose. Maybe the locket was broken all along? Maybe this was all a fool's mission? Or another of Macawber's lies?

No. I didn't travel all the way here to fail now.

'You can do it, Ellari,' I shout.

She shakes her head wildly. 'I can't! Nothing's happening!'

'It has to!' I rack my brains, trying to remember Lord Macawber's words in the laboratory . . . 'Your father said you had the blood, his blood. . .'

Ellari frowns for a second, then bites her finger hard, breaking the skin with her teeth.

She presses her bloodstained finger to the locket and it stutters into life, responding to the magic inside her with a soft glowing. The golden light spreads across the ground like a warm blanket and I gasp . . .

27

'HUMAN! GET HER!' Wrath bellows to his army, pointing out Ellari's position with one taloned finger.

The light from the locket goes out.

Ellari opens her eyes to see the monsters now racing towards her, the only human left in the City.

Terror locks her in its grasp.

'ELLARI!' I shout. 'You can do this!'

Her eyes find mine, I find a tiny glimmer of a smile for her and she nods, closes her eyes again, and this time the locket in her hand doesn't just glow, it burns.

Light floods the City and the monsters approaching her fall, collapsing in heaps, empty husks without their magic. It's working.

The locket is working.

More monsters start to fall, released from their bondage.

I hold a trembling Tingle and Sherman in my arms. 'I love you. I love you. Thank you for being my friends,' I whisper into their ears, my heart breaking into jagged pieces. I don't want to die. I don't.

'Brat!' Molly skids her way towards me and throws herself at me, wrapping her arms around us all. 'I'm sorry, Brat. I won't let you die alone. I won't.'

Connor comes chasing after her and now we're all in a pile on the ground hugging while the army falls around us.

I savour the feeling of being safe and warm and loved even if it is for just a minute. If this is my last memory then it is a good one. The best.

'NOOOOO!!!' Wrath's fury at the sudden destruction of his army fills the square.

He charges at Ellari, his powerful frame throbbing with rage and purpose.

Her eyes are closed and creatures are falling all around her.

He'll fall too. He will. How can he not?

But he's getting closer and closer and . . .

'Ellari!' I scream but it's too late.

Wrath smashes Ellari to the floor, snatches the locket from her grasp, and mangles it into a twisted lump of metal.

The light goes out for good, our one chance to defeat the monsters is gone in a heartbeat but a traitorous burst of joy fills me nonetheless.

Wrath lifts his arms and roars his victory to the skies, the dozen or so monsters still alive join in and the cacophony rises up . . . up . . . up . . .

And then the dome shudders at the tremendous noise and with a sudden crunch it starts to fall, huge pieces shattering on the ground.

28

Chaos rules, the City is a nightmarish place of fleeing monsters and smashing glass.

'RUN!' Connor shouts and he pulls me and Molly to our feet. I race towards Ellari and drag her upright. She's dazed and bleeding but she finds the strength to join us as we dash towards the stores.

Tingle climbs on my shoulders to save her feet from the shards and she warns me where the glass is falling so I can find the safest path.

The remaining monsters are falling beneath the huge panes but still we race. I can't quite believe we're still here, still alive, but if we are then I'm going to do my best to stay that way. To live.

Behind me, Connor has snatched up

Sherman, and Molly is helping Ellari. We can see the entrance to the stores just ahead.

A bull-headed lionus charges at us, bellowing and vicious with fear. I swerve to avoid it and a huge shard of glass smashes down onto the monster, crushing it flat.

There can't be many monsters left now. Between the locket and the dome, the army's been all but destroyed. I start to think we might actually have a chance. A future.

Tingle squeals and I see the shard a second too late. It shatters at my feet, spraying me with glass and very nearly slicing me in half.

I'm left breathless and pocked with glass but still alive. Just.

'Quick,' Connor says, yanking the storeroom door open and flinging Sherman inside. 'Get in before we're all crushed.'

I glance up and see huge gaps in the dome where the glass has fallen but the biggest pieces still remain, teetering on the brink of collapse.

Ellari and Molly rush through the door, Tingle and I follow behind and Connor slams it shut, pulling the crossbar in place.

We take a few breaths to recover but there are still monsters out there and even two or three are enough to kill us and everyone else.

'Come on!' Connor says, herding us all onto the loading platform. Tingle slashes at the rope with her claws and we slam down to the bottom and stagger off.

The shelves have been ravaged by the fleeing refugees, they're all but empty. Only stray apples and crushed biscuits litter the floor as we pelt through on our way to the water control room and our escape.

Ellari skids to a stop suddenly and stares.

'Ellari? What is it?' I turn to see what's caught her eye. Lord Karush is roaming between the shelves; he's holding a jar of preserved peaches and muttering under his breath about the mess.

'It won't do,' he says. 'All this mess. It just won't do.'

The shock has addled his brain.

'Leave him!' Connor calls from up ahead. 'He's not worth it.'

Ellari bites her lip. 'Lord Karush!' she calls. 'It's time to go, come on!'

He ignores her.

A huge slamming thump hits the roof above and the whole cavern trembles and shakes. Small pieces of rock tumble onto our heads.

The last of the dome must have fallen.

With any luck it should have killed the final monsters outside, which means we're finally free of the threat that has plagued us.

We all look up; exhausted, covered in rock dust, and close to collapse.

'I think we did it . . .' Molly says, a dazed expression on her face. 'I think we stopped the army.'

A flood of relief and happiness fills me, and then Molly throws herself into my arms and squeezes me so tightly I think I might break.

'I said you weren't a monster, didn't I Brat? Didn't I?' she says over and over.

'So what now?' Ellari asks. 'We travel down the river to Arberra and then start again? A new life on the outside?'

'A new life,' I repeat, still shocked at my sudden change of fate.

'A new life together,' Molly says.

'Let's get going then,' Connor says. 'I've

had enough of this place.'

'I can't just leave him though,' Ellari says, looking back at Lord Karush.

'Ellari, he's responsible for casting out most of the people out there, do you really think he'll be welcome?' Connor asks.

'No, but I still think we need to start our new lives by doing good, by looking after each other instead of turning our backs,' Ellari says.

Connor sighs and nods. 'All right then. A new start it is.'

She smiles at him and hurries back to get Karush.

Another tremble rocks us. I'm surprised there's any roof left to fall.

'Meanie stinker, Brat!' Tingle whispers in my ear.

'No, it's just more of the dome falling,' I tell her.

'No, Brat-Brat. Look!'

I turn around and see Wrath limping his way through the cavern. The stitching on one of his arms has come loose and it hangs uselessly at his side. His back and face are bleeding and broken from the falling glass but his injuries only make him look even more terrifying than usual.

'You destroyed my army with your magic but there is no escape from me!' he roars at Ellari, spittle flying from his mouth. 'DEATH IS COMING FOR YOU!'

Wrath lurches towards her, claws out, fangs gleaming, determined to end her once and for all.

She watches him come, stiff and frozen with terror.

'Ellari!' I shout her name but she still doesn't move. Can't move, I suspect.

Wrath swings his giant fist at her with every ounce of anger in him but Karush, in some kind of mad act of bravery, shoves her out of the way and takes the full hit to his head. He crumples to the ground, not moving at all.

'Ellari! Run!' Molly screams and with one last, anguished glance at Karush she scrambles to her feet and runs towards us.

We all turn and bolt for the door, our brief hint of safety ripped away.

29

Connor gets to the door first and wrenches it open. Molly flies in next with Sherman, then Tingle, and then me.

We wait for Ellari, her face a horrified blur as she races to get through.

I grab her hand and yank her inside, then Connor slams the door and slides a lock into place. The heavy smash of Wrath's body comes half a second later, rocking the door on its hinges.

'It won't hold him,' I say. The door is thick metal but even so. 'He'll get through. He'll follow us. We'll just lead him right back to everyone else!'

'What else can we do?' Molly asks, her voice high-pitched with panic.

'Can we block the door with something?' Connor suggests.

'There are some barrels over there,' I say, pointing at the corner. 'They must have left them for us. They'll slow him down a little, won't they?'

'Worth a try.'

Molly, Ellari, and I roll the four large barrels over to the door and Connor stacks them two by two against the door.

'It's not going to be enough!' Connor says as the door shakes and shudders, but there's nothing else we can use. The room's full of pipes and nothing else.

'Wait.' I look at the barrels and the markings on them. 'What's inside these?'

'Oil. Leviathan oil. I smuggled it in myself!'

'Oil is flammable, isn't it? Ellari could set it on fire? That might slow him down enough that he won't be able to follow us at least? He could miss the entrance to the well in Arberra and then he'll be following the river for miles . . .'

'It's our best chance,' Connor agrees with a sharp nod. 'Well done, Brat. If we get some cloth we can put it in the opening and light it. If it's long enough that will give us time enough to get away before it goes up.'

We start ripping at our clothes to the sound of Wrath's furious pounding. Molly ties the long pieces together into a rough rope and Connor pulls out a cork from the top barrel and slides the end inside.

'OK good . . . now roll the rest away . . .'

The lock gives suddenly with the next pound and Wrath's taloned hand slips through the gap, his claws slicing straight through Connor's shoulder. He screams in pain but yanks his shoulder free and away from the door.

'Quick!' I shout. Molly and Ellari help me push back at the door and we just about manage to stop Wrath getting further in.

'NO ESCAPE!' Wrath yells. 'Soon you DIE!'

Tingle leaps up on the barrels and slashes at Wrath's hand with her claws. He hisses and yanks his hand away and Sherman's added weight is just enough to get the door closed again.

'Pa!' Molly yells. 'Are you all right, Pa?'

Connor swears and staggers to his feet, his

wound wet with blood. My heart pounds at the thought of losing him now.

Ellari rushes to his side and presses a hand to his shoulder, stemming the blood flow with her magic.

'Go!' I shout at them, needing them to be safe. 'Get down to the river, quick!'

'But I have to light the fuse!' Ellari says.

'Just go!'

Ellari helps Connor limp towards the back where the entrance to the river waits.

The door thuds again. Wrath is losing patience.

'Get me that pipe!' I tell Molly, pointing at a broken one in the corner. She yanks it off and hands it to me.

I wedge it under the handle and into the corner as hard as I can. It will buy us a few more minutes.

'You go Molly. You need to be with your dad.'

'But . . . how will you . . . ?'

'I can do this Molly. Trust me!'

She bites her lip. 'You're not going to do anything . . . stupid, are you?'

'I swear! No more sacrifices, not this time.'

'Good. Because if you die now I'm going to kill you, got it?'

'Got it.'

She runs away after Ellari and her pa and now it's all down to me. I'm not afraid though. A small, brand-new seed of self-belief sits firmly in my heart.

'Right. Tingle, Sherman, we need to make a spark. Find me a stone or something sharp.'

'Tingle's claws are sharp!' she says, unsheathing one paw.

'That might work. Can you scratch something hard? The floor? Try that.'

Tingle slashes at the stone floor a few times but nothing happens.

The door starts to splinter.

I stay calm. It's going to be all right. I back away from the door, unwinding the cloth rope as I go.

'Something else, Tingle, try something else.'

'Sherman's shell?' she suggests.

'Yes! Try that. Come on, Sherman.'

We're all ready. The cloth is unwound.

The open hatch is just behind us and the door is about to give way. All we need is a spark.

'Now, Tingle!'

She scrapes her claws over Sherman's shell; once, twice, three times and nothing.

My belly starts to tense. What if we can't do it? What if my plan fails? Molly's going to kill me!

Four times, five times . . . a spark! I catch it on the cloth and blow very gently. The spark grows into a tiny flame and the fire races along the rope towards the barrels of oil.

The pipe wedging the door falls. Wrath smashes his way through the top of the door.

'You cannot escape death, boy!' Wrath bellows, his huge jaws bright with razor-sharp teeth.

The flame reaches the barrel.

'I've done it before!' I shout. 'Just watch me!'

He roars his rage at me but I don't care.

I grab Tingle and Sherman and throw myself backwards through the hole as the barrels explode into flame and the entire room turns bright red and gold. A rush of wind slams me down into the platform below and my head hits the wood so hard I'm seeing stars.

'Brat . . . Brat!' Molly's voice is frantic but darkness creeps up on me and snatches me away before I can answer.

30

'Brat-Brat?'

I open my eyes, squinting at the light.

Tingle immediately licks my eyeball and I squeal and push her away.

'Brat-Brat wake up! Brat-Brat sleep too long. Tingle lonely.'

Confused and aching, I open my eyes again and sit up carefully.

I am, it seems, alive. And so is Tingle. And, judging from the snoring at the end of the bed, so is Sherman.

You don't get licked on the eyeball when you're dead, do you?

My bed is a narrow mattress on a wooden frame, the walls around me are made of grey skin and cloth, and a soft sea breeze fills the air.

'Where are we?' I ask, my voice hoarse.

'We stay with Molly! Molly give Tingle very nice munchies and lots of strokes but Tingle still love Brat the mostest.'

I smile and run my hand over her soft fur. She's solid, real, not a dream.

Sherman wakes up, yawns, and plods his way up the bed so he can flop down on my chest. 'Molly not scratch as good as Brat.'

I rub under his shell with my other hand and his chest rumbles with appreciation.

'Brat?'

I look up, it's Ellari. She looks good, her face flushed with colour, her hair loose and tousled by the wind. 'Thank the stars, I thought you were never going to wake up.'

'So did I.'

'Well, you were lucky I was there. You hit your head quite badly when you landed on the jetty. I've done my best but it will take a while for you to heal properly.'

'Wrath?' I ask.

'Gone. The War Creatures. The City. All of it.'

A massive wave of relief washes over me.

'It's all thanks to you, Brat.'

'Don't be silly. I didn't do much.'

'Yes, you did Brat. You saved us all. We'd all be dead without you and we won't forget it.'

I can feel my cheeks flush at her kind words. A small sense of pride fills me.

'Tingle done good too!' Tingle says, jumping up and down on the bed.

'Yes you did! You were brilliant!' I tell her. Tingle puffs out her chest.

'And so was Sherman!' I continue. 'And Molly and Ellari and everyone! I can't believe you managed to get us all back to the village.'

'Well,' Molly says, marching in. 'You didn't really think we'd leave you behind, did you? Even if you did scare me half to death with that explosion!'

'I'm sorry. I didn't know it was going to explode like that!'

'Well, I suppose I can forgive you,' she says, beaming a big smile at me.

'How long have I been asleep?' I ask.

'A few days. We had to drag you through the river but there were lots of people to help pull you up into Arberra. My ma was waiting there with half the village. They helped carry you back here to our village on a stretcher.'

'Really?'

'Yes, I think they felt guilty for leaving so they came to help,' Molly says, a hint of pride in her voice.

'How are the rest of the survivors coping?'

Molly rolls her eyes. 'I've never known people moan so much but I think they're settling in. Every village on the coast has taken some people in and we've shared out the supplies from the City. Best of all though, Ellari's planning to add her magic to the compost my ma makes, and with so many gardeners among the survivors we think we'll be able to get a few crops in the ground this year if we work hard enough.'

'I really think we can heal this scorched earth eventually, Brat, all thanks to you,' Ellari says, smiling down at me.

'Oi!' Connor says, barging his way through, one arm wrapped in a sling. 'No one told me our young hero had woken up!'

I beam at him. 'Connor! You're all right!'

'Thanks to Ellari I am. She kept us both

alive you know.'

Ellari blushes. 'Well, I knew Molly would kill me if I didn't!'

Connor laughs. 'You're not wrong there!'

'What?' Molly demands. 'I need to keep my family in one piece!' she says. 'One pa and one brother.'

She smiles at me and I can feel my heart swell.

'Really, Molly?'

'Really, you big barnacle head.'

'I always wanted a son,' Connor says to me, ruffling my hair. 'Girls are nothing but trouble you know.'

'Oi! I'll show you trouble if you're not careful!' Molly says, but she's laughing and so am I.

'Can we go to the party now?' Tingle demands.

'What party?' I ask. 'Where?'

'On the beach! Ellari hoped you might wake up today. We're having a small party, loads of food, a little bit of moonshine, and plenty of fun,' Connor says.

'Oh, I'm not sure . . .' Suddenly I feel shy

and nervous.

'No getting out of it, Brat. You're the guest of honour!' Molly adds.

'But . . .'

'No arguments. We've been waiting a long time for you to wake up!'

Kendrick appears in the tent, gruff as ever but bearing a small smile for me. He scoops me up in my blankets with Tingle and Sherman clinging on and carries me outside where everyone is waiting around a huge fire.

The smell of fresh fish and bread and potatoes and apples, all baking in the coals, sets my tummy grumbling.

As I get nearer, everyone stands up and starts clapping.

I think my heart might burst with all the feelings. So many people here, so many good friends, family even, and a chance of a proper future.

They all raise their cups to me.

'To Brat!' they shout, drinking deeply.

'And Tingle!' she shouts, making everyone laugh and drink again.

Kendrick settles me down next to the fire

and Cassy brings me a heaped plate of food. I even manage to eat some before Tingle and Sherman get to it.

Ellari comes to sit next to me and I let the question that's been bothering me come out.

'You know when you used the locket?'

'Yes?'

'Well . . . I was just wondering if you knew how come some of the monsters didn't fall? How come we didn't fall?'

She tilts her head as she considers. 'It was strange actually . . . some of the creatures fell easily, as soon as the light touched them, as if they were glad to go. But a few were bonded much more firmly to life and managed to hold on . . . maybe they had a stronger reason to stay?'

I nod. That makes sense. 'Wrath's reason was rage and revenge I think.'

'And yours?'

'Hope,' I say and she smiles at me.

'The strongest reason of all.'

I watch the sun sinking over the sea, letting the happy hum of chatter and song wash over me. The monsters are finally all gone. Even the ones inside me that told me I was no good, that I was useless.

I'm ready to start my new life. The one I barely hoped for. The one I know I deserve.

ACKNOWLEDGEMENTS

This book owes a huge debt to my wonderful editor Clare Whitston who guided me patiently through countless drafts in order to find the heart and soul hiding underneath.

Much love and gratitude goes to my agent Kate Shaw who never stops believing in me.

Huge and enormous thanks to all my wonderful friends, especially—

Jude—Always and forever babes. James and Vashti—not sure what I'd do without you. Jen—I'm so lucky to have you! My wife Miriam—love you always. Gail—a star and an angel all rolled into one.

Special thanks go—

To Peter for reading and providing such a lovely cover quote.

To my crit group and all the UKMGCHATTERS, Eggs and SCBWI's who have supported me!

To all the wonderful librarians, teachers and booksellers who get books like mine into the hands of children, but especially to Nicki Cleveland, Jo Clarke, Zoe, and Natasha and Jim at Chicken and Frog bookshop.

To my mum and dad who never stop supporting me even when they are struggling. Love you both so much.

To Luke for providing much needed hugs, occasional brainstorming sessions, and never ending love.

And to Pickle and Boots—the inspiration behind Tingle and Sherman!

ABOUT THE AUTHOR

Raised by an Austrian mother and Indian father on a concrete council estate in east London, Lorraine spent most of her childhood escaping into the imaginary worlds of books by Dahl, Lindgren and Blyton or creating her own sprawling, adventuresome stories.

Her dreams of becoming a writer were abandoned when the boring trappings of adulthood ensnared her and convinced her to give up what seemed to be an impossible dream. Instead she trained as a chef, married, became a mother and then retrained as an antenatal teacher. It was only when her young son couldn't find anything he wanted to read that she began to write again.

Now she spends her days writing fantasy books for children, surrounded by her family and two fluffy cats, occasionally venturing out to teach, see friends or shop for more books!

Her first book, *Mold and the Poison Plot*, was the winner of the SCWBI Crystal Kite Award.

He's got a BIG heart... and a NOSE to match!

MOLD AND THE POISON PLOT

LORRAINE GREGORY

Mold's a bit of a freak. His nose is as big as his body is puny and his mother abandoned him in a bin when he was a mere baby. Who else but the old healer, Aggy, would have taken him in and raised him as her own? But when Aggy is accused of poisoning the King, Mold sets out to clear her name.

In a thrilling race against time to save Aggy from the hangman's noose, Mold faces hideous, deadly monsters like the Yurg and the Purple Narlo Frog. He finds true friendship in the most unusual—and smelly—of places and must pit his wits and his clever nose against the evil witch Hexaba.

Ready for more great stories?
Try one of these...

JULIA GREEN

To the Edge of the World

A new life. A fearless friend. A wild sea adventure.

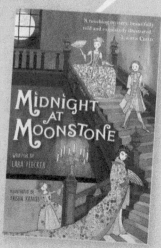

'A touching mystery, beautifully told and exquisitely illustrated' Laura Carlin

MIDNIGHT AT MOONSTONE

WRITTEN BY LARA FLECKER

ILLUSTRATED BY TRISHA KRAUSS

CERRIE BURNELL

The GIRL with the SHARK'S TEETH

Can a girl who is lost on land find answers in the Wild Deep?

THE Closest Thing to Flying

TWO GIRLS A CENTURY APART. TOGETHER THEY'LL FIND FREEDOM

GILL LEWIS